I0623106

ABOUT THIS BOOK

Welcome to Havenwood Falls, a small town in the majestic mountains of Colorado. A town where legacies began centuries ago, bloodlines run deep, and dark secrets abound. A town where nobody is what you think, where truths pose as lies, and where myths blend with reality. A place where everyone has a story. This is only but one . . .

Aster McCabe couldn't be happier with her job managing Coffee Haven and baking blueberry scones the whole town raves about, especially her sweet and sexy boyfriend Patrick. She loves her simple, small-town life in Havenwood Falls. At least, until her sister suddenly shows up with trouble not far behind.

The sisters' relationship has always been volatile, especially with the pressure of being the alpha's daughters and the expectation to be perfect. Reeve never failed in that department, and Aster grew up in the shadow of her sister's success. But when Reeve left for college, Aster blossomed. So she's dealt a painful blow the moment her sister walks in the door and meets Patrick—a mountain lion's call to its mate couldn't be any more obvious. Neither can it be controlled or refused.

When an unstable alpha from another den claims Reeve as his mate, Aster, bitter over the recent betrayal, practically draws the guy a map to Reeve's location, unknowingly putting her entire family and den in danger. Aster must figure out how to right her wrong and save her family. But loyalty and love are further tested when a stranger appears with the potential to forever change Aster's fate.

FATE, LOVE & LOYALTY

A HAVENWOOD FALLS NOVELLA

E.J. FECHENDA

HAVENWOOD FALLS BOOKS

Forget You Not by Kristie Cook

Old Wounds by Susan Burdorf

Fate, Love & Loyalty by E.J. Fechenda

Covetousness by Randi Cooley Wilson

The Winged & the Wicked by T.V. Hahn & Kristie Cook

Alpha's Queen by Lila Felix

Ink & Fire by R.K. Ryals

More books releasing on a monthly basis

Also try the YA series, Havenwood Falls High

Stay up to date at www.HavenwoodFalls.com

BOOKS BY E.J. FECHENDA

The New Mafia Trilogy

The Beautiful People

Clean Slate

Endings & Beginnings

Enforcer (a prequel novella)

The Ghost Stories Trilogy

End of the Road

Havoc

Copyright © 2017 E.J. Fechenda, Ang'dora Productions, LLC

All rights reserved.

Published by

Ang'dora Productions, LLC

5621 Strand Blvd, Ste 210

Naples, FL 34110

Havenwood Falls and Ang'dora Productions and their associated logos are trademarks and/or registered trademarks of Ang'dora Productions, LLC.

Cover design by Regina Wamba at MaeIDesign.com

Except as permitted under the U.S. Copyright Act of 1976, no part of this publication may be reproduced, stored in a retrieval system, or transmitted in any form or by any means, electronic, mechanical, photocopying, recording, or otherwise, without written permission of the owner of this book.

Please do not participate in or encourage piracy of copyrighted materials in violation of the author's rights. Purchase only authorized editions.

This book is a work of fiction. Names, characters, and events are either products of the author's imagination or are used fictitiously, and any resemblance to actual persons, living or dead, is entirely coincidental.

Ebook ISBN: 978-1-939859-34-1

Print ISBN: 978-1-939859-45-7

This book is dedicated to Annette and Carrie. You may have lost your battles this year, but you fought until the end. You taught me to not take anything for granted and to persist, no matter what.

CHAPTER 1

*T*he bell above the front door chimed, and Aster McCabe looked up from the espresso machine, anticipating her boyfriend since she'd been counting down the minutes all morning. They were going away to celebrate their six-month anniversary with a long overdue trip to her family's cabin located in a remote area in the mountains. There they'd be able to shift and run and hunt together, away from the watchful eyes of the community. With Patrick being new to the den and new to Havenwood Falls, there were some who viewed his attachment to Aster as more of a strategic political move. Being the alpha's daughter placed Aster and anyone she became involved with under more scrutiny—a fact that she hated. She always felt she was being held to a higher standard than the other members of their den, and her perfect sister, Reeve, had raised the standards even higher. At the thought of her sister, Aster scowled. The last time Reeve had been home was for Christmas, right before Patrick had shown up in town, and they'd fought constantly.

Instead of Patrick, Aster's boss, Willow Fairchild, walked in cradling her swollen belly—the reason why she'd been showing up later and later for work. A gust of wind followed her in, carrying the sweet fragrance from catalpa trees that were in full bloom. The town square across the street was home to several of these towering trees, which had more fluffy white blossoms than leaves.

"How are you feeling?" Aster asked, deftly steaming milk without even looking at the machine.

"Good. Tired. The baby kicked up a storm last night." Willow eased into a chair at one of the few empty tables near the front counter.

"I can cancel my weekend away if you're not up to running the shop," Aster offered as she handed a latte to a waiting customer.

"No, no. You and Patrick have been planning this. I'll be fine, and Paisley is able to work some extra hours." Willow dismissed Aster with a wave of her hand before resting it back on top of her baby bump. With her white-blonde hair and pixie features, Willow looked barely old enough to be pregnant. While her fae heritage gifted her with a youthful appearance, she was really six years older than Aster. After Aster graduated from college in December, Willow promoted her to manager—a timely decision, since Willow found out a month later that she was pregnant.

Shadows under Willow's eyes, more noticeable because of her porcelain skin, made Aster worry. What if she left and something bad happened? Willow had become more like the sister she wanted, and Aster suddenly felt guilty about leaving. Was it selfish of her to go? She attempted to shrug off the negative thoughts, but it was too late. Willow had already received them. It was hard to hide anything from her boss, one of Havenwood Falls' most powerful empaths. She sensed emotions from miles away.

"Stop it, Aster," Willow said. "You worry too much about what other people think. You need to get out of here and let loose—it will do you some good."

Aster smiled and smoothed her apron, wiping at a clump of flour from a batch of her blueberry scones that won Best of Havenwood Falls two years in a row. Streaks of white powder stood out against the black fabric. "I know."

Willow's command was easier said than done. Having grown up in Reeve's shadow, Aster had years of feeling insecure holding her back.

Reeve had moved to Denver and had been gone for more than six years, but the comparisons never stopped. Reeve was high school class valedictorian, she was Miss Teen Havenwood Falls, and she practically walked on water. Guys of all species salivated in her wake. Back then, Aster had been an awkward teenager, and puberty hadn't been kind. All knobby knees and elbows with carrot-orange hair that stuck out in a riot of uncontrollable curls, she was a far cry from beautiful Reeve. She was even envious that her sister was able to leave Havenwood Falls to move to the city, where she lived a glamorous life. Of course, the Court of the Sun and the Moon, the governing body for supes in town, made an exception for her and lifted the spell that usually made other supes and humans forget their time spent in Havenwood Falls.

"You're doing it again." Willow's voice broke through Aster's thoughts. "Have you heard from Reeve?"

"Not lately. She's probably busy planning some extravagant event for some celebrity." Aster turned around to open the oven door. Heat blasted her skin, and the sweet aroma of blueberries and cinnamon assaulted her nostrils. She grabbed an oven mitt and pulled out a tray of golden-brown scones, setting them on the marble counter to cool. She loved the old-fashioned counter and that she didn't have to worry about using a cooling rack or hot pad.

"Aster, you have carved out your own life here and landed an awesome job with the coolest boss ever. Oh, and you have a hot piece of man meat. Who knows, soon you could be sporting one of these." Willow patted her baby bump dramatically, making Aster laugh.

"No! Hell no! I'm not ready for that." Aster shook her head in denial, her ponytail swishing along her back with the movement. Her once carrot-orange hair had darkened to a light auburn, and the longer she grew it, the more the curls relaxed. These days she had grown to appreciate her locks, but had to keep them pulled back. No one appreciated hair in their scones. While she disagreed with Willow on babies, she did agree with her about having an awesome job.

Aster surveyed the shop, taking a moment to admire all of her hard work over the past year. Paintings from local artists hung on the red brick walls, adding color to the space. At Aster's suggestion, Willow had added flower boxes to the large front picture window, and the wildflowers that bloomed were a cheerful greeting to anyone walking by outside. Several hanging plants inside, along with Willow's crystal collection, added a quirky vibe. Overall, the effect was relaxing and inviting. Combined with the good coffee and food, Coffee Haven was a favorite among locals and visitors.

"Well, it's going to happen one of these days, because you're a catch. Why do you think eighty-five percent of our customers are male?" Willow winked, because at that moment Patrick walked in the door. "And all of them are hot for you. Feelings . . . I pick up on these things, you know," she said and tapped her temple.

"Who's hot for you, besides me?" Patrick said with a growl. He stalked across the shop and around the counter, pulling Aster into his arms. She sank into his warmth and breathed in his musk. He rubbed his cheeks against her hair, an instinctual way of marking her with his scent. She tilted her head up, and he slanted his mouth over hers, sending the message to any male in the coffee shop that she was taken. This sent a shiver through her, though she never would have admitted the whole display of male dominance turned her on. Of course, Willow picked up on it and started to giggle. Aster flipped her off behind Patrick's back, which made Willow laugh even harder.

"You ready to go, babe?" Patrick asked when they separated.

"Yes," she responded breathlessly. "My bag is upstairs."

One of the perks of being manager of the coffee shop was the apartment upstairs, which Willow rented to her at a reduced rate, since having a mountain lion shifter living upstairs was added security. Aster untied her apron and tossed it in the hamper under the sink.

Just as they were preparing to leave, the bell above the door chimed. Aster turned to see who was coming in and froze in place. *What the hell was Reeve doing here?* There her sister stood, wearing simple jeans and a black T-shirt, but still managing to showcase every curve. Her hair looked like she had just had it professionally styled; auburn waves framed her heart-shaped face. While Aster was momentarily stunned, Patrick was not, and she watched in disbelief as he prowled toward Reeve.

"Patrick?" Aster called, and she reached for his arm, but he shrugged her off. "Patrick!" she said louder, and he looked back at her briefly with a dazed look in his eyes.

He blinked once, slowly, before focusing on Reeve again. Aster stared in disbelief as she noticed Reeve's dreamy expression and how her sister tracked Patrick's every move. Then she realized what was happening, and her stomach dropped to her toes. She'd seen this before, when their brother Braden met his wife, Kaitlyn.

"Oh, shit," Willow said from behind the counter, and Aster looked at her. "I'm so sorry, honey." Her bright blue eyes shone with sympathy.

Willow's confirmation hit Aster like a punch in the gut, and she bent over as if in physical pain. She couldn't breathe and couldn't process what was happening. Reeve wasn't even supposed to be there in the first place.

"Unbelievable!" she screamed. "You always get everything. Why?"

She couldn't bear to look at them anymore as they scented each other and began touching every inch of exposed skin, oblivious to anyone else around them. With a sob, Aster stormed out through the back of the shop. As soon as she was in the alley behind Coffee Haven, she stripped off her clothes, shifted into her cat form, and took off for the woods on the outskirts of town. She didn't care that running through town as a mountain lion was frowned upon or that there would be consequences. All she cared about was running far away from her sister before she did something stupid, like gouge her eyes out with her claws . . . or kill her.

CHAPTER 2

*F*or Reeve McCabe, meeting her true mate couldn't have come at a worst time. She wanted to fight it, but was powerless against the attraction. She felt inexplicably drawn to the handsome stranger in the coffee shop, and he became her only focus. She smelled her sister's scent all over him, and it made her want to pounce on him to claim him right then and there. Aster. The only reason she stopped by the coffee shop to begin with. She broke away from her mate's gaze when her sister cried out and winced when she saw the hurt on Aster's flushed face, her red cheeks stained with tears. When Aster took off, Reeve ran after her.

She called out for Aster to come back, but by the time she reached the alley, Aster was gone, her clothes a discarded heap on the pavement. Reeve started to call her cat forward so she could pursue her sister, but her cat had nothing but mating on her mind and refused to cooperate. She was unable to leave her mate. She didn't even know his name or where he came from, but that didn't matter. Now that they'd crossed paths, she knew she'd never stray far from his side.

She had come to tell Aster she was home for an indefinite amount of time. Life had gone sideways in Denver, and she needed the security, the protection, of the den and her family. Trouble had followed Reeve lately, and sadness weighed heavy on her heart when she realized the source of her sister's anguish. Her mate was Aster's boyfriend. Shit. Without even meaning to, she had once again caused her sister pain. With a sigh, Reeve picked up her sister's clothes and folded them. She brought them inside and left them in a neat stack on top of a cardboard box before returning to her mate.

"I feel just as shitty, too. Aster doesn't deserve this. She's a good person. I've seen you in the pictures she has in her apartment. You're Reeve?" her mate asked in a deep voice that echoed within her soul. He brushed a tear off of her cheek before his hands came to rest on her hips, and she felt the strength they possessed. His eyes were a warm brown, framed with thick lashes. His light brown hair was long on top and tousled. A straight nose brought her attention to his full lips.

"Yes," she replied and stepped closer so their bodies were a breath apart. "And you are?" His heart pounded a strong, steady beat, and she was shocked to discover her heartbeat had already aligned with his.

"Patrick O'Shea." A hand left her hip and ghosted up her side, lightly brushing against her right breast before cupping her cheek. She leaned into his touch and purred. All thoughts of anything except Patrick disappeared when he touched her. She knew they had an audience in the coffee shop, but she didn't care. The instinct to fully mate with Patrick clouded her brain. "Please tell me you have your own place, because I'm staying with my parents."

Patrick smiled, his canines already grown longer, and his eyes flashed golden. "I do. Let's go."

They quickly left Coffee Haven, a boatload of pheromones following them out the door.

Patrick lived in Havenwood Village, an apartment complex located a block away from downtown Main Street. At the speed they ran, they reached his apartment within minutes. He opened the front door, and that's as far as they got. Patrick pressed her up against the wall and lowered his head to capture her lips. She tilted to meet him and growled in appreciation when they connected. His lips were soft, but the kiss was hard with urgency. She parted her mouth and welcomed his tongue while burying her hands in his thick hair and tugging on it, encouraging him to deepen the kiss. Reeve moved her hips forward, and as if in sync, Patrick did too. His arousal pressed against her belly, and she broke off the kiss.

"I can't believe this is really happening," she panted.

"Me either," Patrick said between kisses that he traced from the corner of her mouth and along her neck. She tilted her head back, giving him more access. He brushed her long auburn hair behind her shoulder and gently bit down on at the juncture of her neck and shoulder. His canines just barely broke the skin. The act of dominance triggered waves of lust.

"Wait, I don't even know you, and what about Aster?" she asked, trying to retain a grip on reality and not be consumed by her emotions. Reeve's voice shook as she struggled to form the words.

Patrick groaned, but raised his head to meet her gaze with glowing eyes, his irises darker slits, echoing her struggle for control as his cat called to hers. "Trust me, Aster needs her space, and honestly, I don't think I can stop. We will get to know each other—we have our entire lives to learn everything there is to know and so much more."

He kissed her again, and Reeve allowed her cat closer to the surface. She shifted enough to allow her hands to transform into paws tipped with sharp claws, and she shredded Patrick's shirt. He growled with approval, his eyes flashing golden again right before he sliced her shirt open with an equally sharp set of claws. Soon their shredded clothes lay in a pile on the floor, and they stood naked before each other without any shyness.

Reeve admired her mate, running a hand down his muscular chest and stomach. He had a few scars on his side—faint claw marks that had faded to white—which she guessed were from an old injury. Leaning forward, she gently licked the scars, then placed a soft kiss on his skin. His scent filled her nose, and her whole body pulsed with a powerful wave of arousal. She gasped and stood up straight, almost dizzy with need. Patrick looked her over appreciatively, and her skin flushed under his gaze. His nostrils flared, and his eyes glowed amber right before he spun Reeve around so she faced the wall.

"I don't have the patience to be gentle or slow, but I promise the next time . . ." He ran his nose along her neck and cupped her breasts from behind. She arched her back and pressed into his hands. With every touch, she felt her hold on reality slipping, her conscience suppressed by the call to mate. Every nerve in her body hummed with promise and came alive with each caress.

She whimpered as she stopped resisting. "Take me. I'm yours."

The moment he entered her, Reeve knew there would never be another man for her. Their souls merged, and she felt his need as acutely as her own. His hard, muscular body pressed her against the wall, and she pushed back against him, causing him to drive deeper.

"Oh my God," Reeve cried out, and her knees threatened to go soft.

Patrick brushed her hair aside and bit down on her neck. This time his teeth pierced her skin, completing his claim on her. An overwhelming sense of peace and pleasure consumed her as she felt her blood surging into his mouth. With a final thrust and grunt, Patrick stilled and rode out her orgasm while licking the bite mark clean. They stayed pressed against each other, their pulses pounding, for a few moments, catching their breaths. Reeve slowly turned around to face her mate. His hair stuck out in all directions, and his cheeks were flushed from exertion. Reeve wrapped her arms around his neck and stood on her tiptoes, pulling him to her for a kiss. Now that the initial itch had been scratched, the urgency had waned, but after a few strokes of her tongue, Patrick was ready again.

This time they faced each other. She raised a leg and hooked it over his hip, and he slid inside. They moved in sync, creating a rhythm that quickly rose to a crescendo. Patrick lifted her up, so she wrapped her legs around him. From this angle, she was at the right height to stake her claim. She licked the spot on his neck first, and the vein pulsed underneath her tongue. Her canines dropped, and she struck, drawing his blood into her mouth. The iron-rich warmth bubbled up, and she drank deeply until Patrick released with a muffled groan. Then she retracted her teeth and licked the wound. She was his, and he was hers. The mating bond was officially complete, and there was no going back.

After they collapsed in Patrick's bed, sated and drowsy, the guilt set in.

"I don't regret finding you, my mate," Patrick said as they lay in his dark bedroom. "But I just hate that Aster is hurt. I do care for her, but now, you're all I can see."

"I know. I tried to resist, but the mating call . . . I've never experienced anything so powerful before. Poor Aster." Reeve sighed and rolled over onto her side to face Patrick. He moved so she could settle against him with his arm tucked in behind her, holding her close. "It's not like I planned this. Trust me, I have enough complications in my life, and I just added another reason for my sister to hate me forever."

CHAPTER 3

*A*ster stayed in her cat form all weekend and lost herself in the woods. At first, she ran to the waterfalls, but because it was June and a gorgeous, sunny day, there were too many people around, so she went high up into the mountains. She almost reached the peak, and at 13,000 feet elevation, a significant snow pack from the harsh winter remained on the ground, which meant fewer people. Aster made sure to stay within the 25-mile radius of town, the boundary for the memory ward, one of the protective measures put into place to protect Havenwood Falls' secrets.

Here she roamed along jagged rocks, and when she paused to rest, she stared down at her hometown nestled in the box canyon. Lights twinkled like stars below, and from above, Havenwood Falls appeared even smaller, almost fake, like a diorama. Aster found her escape in the mountains, away from the sometimes suffocating routine of small-town life. Patrick had provided a break from the mundane. He had been new and different and exciting. Before she could dwell on her loss, Aster caught the scent of a deer on the wind.

Going back to nature and giving in to her animal instincts helped to take her mind off of Reeve and Patrick's betrayal, but it didn't take the hurt away. She returned to her apartment early Monday morning.

The sky was still dark, but the chorus of birds that silenced as she slinked through the town's quiet streets let her know dawn was coming. She had followed Mathews River that ran south of Havenwood Falls. Once she passed the ski resort, she cut up Ninth Street, which led right to the shops on Main Street. She stuck to the shadows, where the illumination of street lamps didn't reach, and she ducked behind parked cars or bushes whenever her acute hearing detected somebody nearby.

When she reached the privacy of the alley between Coffee Haven and Callie's Consignments, only then did she shift. Focusing on her human form, she willed her cat to let go and shifted back. She had to stay crouched down until her body adjusted to the transformation. The longer she spent in her cat form, the harder it was to transition. Her animal nature wanted to dominate, and the euphoria from hunting lingered. She shook it off and slowly stood up, adjusting to being bipedal before hurrying up the stairs.

Since she was naked and left her keys inside Coffee Haven, she bent down and lifted up the doormat to retrieve her spare, but it wasn't there. Sniffing the air and doorknob, she figured out who last had entered her apartment, and the visitor was still inside.

Aster opened the door and stepped into the kitchen. Her apartment was dark, but her enhanced vision enabled her to see everything clearly. Her bedroom was just past the kitchen to the left of the hallway, so she stopped there first to put on the pajama pants and camisole top that were still draped on the foot of her bed.

Anne McCabe sat on the futon in the living room, waiting for her. Wordlessly, Aster crossed the room and sunk down next to her mom. She grabbed a throw pillow and hugged it to her chest.

"Willow told me what happened," Anne said. "I'm so sorry, sweetie."

Aster curled her legs up and leaned into the comforting warmth of her mother. Her familiar scent, a combination of sweet honeysuckle and jasmine, helped soothe the ache of Aster's wounded heart. She let out a sob that was quickly followed by another. Soon a full-on crying jag consumed her. Her mom held her close and combed her fingers through Aster's tangled curls while she poured out her bottled-up emotions.

"The hurt will fade, sweetie. Don't be angry at your sister or Patrick. They're powerless against the bond. You know that is something that can't be controlled." Aster sniffed and nodded, hating to acknowledge that her mom spoke the truth. "Someday you'll find your true mate and experience how powerful the connection is, then you'll truly understand."

"I'll never find my mate in Havenwood Falls, or I would have already."

"Hush. You can't know that. Who's to say your mate won't find his way to you?"

This made Aster remember the tales she'd heard growing up, about how mates were pulled toward each other. That didn't explain Patrick's appearance, though, since Reeve didn't live in Havenwood Falls, and she said so to her mom.

"Patrick showed up in January, right?" her mom asked, and Aster confirmed. "Not too long after Reeve left after being home for the holidays. Maybe he was close and felt the pull. It's possible Patrick felt drawn to you since you have similar DNA—a close match, but not a true match. It's happened before."

"Really?" Aster sat up, wiping her tearstained cheeks, and twisted to face her mom.

"You haven't heard about Great Aunt Cordelia?"

"No, I don't think so."

"Great Aunt Cordelia, who you remind me a lot of, had been out for a run up on Pike's Peak when she came across another mountain lion shifter, but he was a stranger. Apparently they had quite the romp in the woods, and he followed Cordelia back to Havenwood Falls. There was a great bonfire party that night by the waterfalls—what we now call the Carnival at the Falls—and practically the whole town was there when Cordelia showed up with her date. Unfortunately, the moment she introduced him to her twin sister, Great Aunt Courtney, well, that's when the true mate bond took hold. Not even a year later, Cordelia was working as a waitress at the Fallview Tavern when a shifter who was on vacation was seated in her section. The handsome stranger turned out to be her true mate."

"Uncle Paul?"

"Yup, and if you ask him, he'll tell you he had never heard of Havenwood Falls before, but the bus he was taking to California from Missouri drove through Grand Junction, and he felt the call of his mate tugging at him from over a hundred miles away, like he had a rope tied around his waist. He ordered the bus driver to let him off and followed his instinct right to the tavern."

"Wow! I had no idea."

"The pull can be very strong. So don't give up hope. Aunt Cordelia didn't talk to her sister for weeks after, and the sting of humiliation lasted longer. It's not just the McCabes who are stubborn," she said with a wink, referring to her mom's side of the family, the Fitzpatricks. "But Cordelia eventually got over it."

Learning about her great aunt's history did provide a spark of hope. All Aster wanted was a close relationship with her sister, and maybe someday it would be possible.

"Thanks for being here, Mom." Aster leaned over and kissed her mom's cheek.

"No problem, sweetie. Now you're probably ready to crash. Go get some rest."

At the mention of sleep, Aster yawned and felt the fatigue from her weekend exertions bearing down on her. Her tired eyes were even scratchier since her crying fit. She walked her mom to the door, and after a hug goodbye, she climbed into bed and immediately fell asleep.

Aster woke a little bit before noon, but not until she showered, brushed her teeth and drank two glasses of water did she start to feel human again. She checked her phone and saw the text from Willow telling her to take the day off. There was a text from her brother as well as some friends, all of them expressing concern for her. Gossip spread fast in Havenwood Falls. She ate a bowl of cereal while checking her email to see if Reeve or Patrick had tried reaching out that way, but they hadn't, and this made her lose her appetite. *Do they not care about me at all that they don't have the decency to check on me after three days?*

She dumped the soggy remains of her cereal in the trash and set her bowl in the sink.

Only an hour had passed since she had showered, and boredom was quickly setting in. Aster walked back into her bedroom to grab a book when she noticed the bag she had packed for the weekend getaway sitting on the floor by the door. Seeing it triggered a powerful wave of anger and sadness, and she kicked it, sending it skidding across the hardwood floor. Knowing she needed a distraction, she went downstairs to throw herself into work.

There were a few people sitting at tables. She said hello to Harlow, a friend and witch who was a member of the Luna Coven. She waved at Caleb, a bear shifter who had just graduated high school. He sat with Nikki and Serena, friends of Willow's cousin, Paisley. The teen girls were twirling their hair and sitting to display their assets. Aster recognized the flirting techniques, and Caleb's rapt expression indicated he wasn't immune to their charms. The poor boy was outnumbered and didn't stand a chance. A couple of dragon shifters sat in the corner with iced coffees dripping condensation on the table. She located Willow behind the counter, taking inventory of baked goods. A few months ago she would have done this task while standing, but now she sat on a stool.

She paused to read a poster taped to the front of the counter by the register that Willow must have put up over the weekend. The poster advertised a book drive fundraiser to help rebuild the library that had burned down.

"Can I help? I can make more blueberry scones," Aster offered, since they were sold out.

Willow looked up at her with a scowl. "Yeah, you can help by taking the day off and getting your head together. I could sense your emo angst from across the room."

"Emo angst?" Aster replied with a laugh. "I think only guys can be emo."

"Well, whatever. Just go away. Take advantage, because once this baby comes you'll be working more."

Aster leaned against the counter and crossed her arms, taking in

Willow's appearance. Her fair skin was flushed, and her brows were furrowed together, creating a crease in an otherwise flawless face.

"What's wrong?"

Willow exhaled, blowing a few wisps of fine blonde hair out of the way. She sat up and rubbed her belly. "I sense danger coming. It's been getting stronger all weekend." Willow looked up at Aster. "I already called Sheriff Kasun to let him know to expect some trouble."

"That bad, huh?"

"Yeah, off the charts. I haven't sensed this much since the vampire massacre of '05."

Aster's eyebrows rose at the significance of the reference. She was only ten years old when Viktor Azimov, the head of the local Gothic vampires, went mad after drinking the blood of a heroin addict. Willow was in high school at the time and coming into her empathic abilities when she sensed the change in Viktor the moment he drank the tainted blood. Willow had told Aster that she didn't know what to do with the emotions she was receiving, and she didn't know who was emitting them, so all she could do was ride out the storm. Viktor decapitated a half dozen of his vampires before he was subdued. Later he was decapitated too, when he was sentenced to meet his true death as punishment for his crimes. Aster shivered at the idea of being at the mercy of the Court.

"Do you know who it is?"

"No, the signature is unfamiliar to me, so it's not someone from Havenwood Falls. Just be on the lookout. I sense the danger is near."

"Okay," Aster promised.

Since Willow refused to let her work, Aster made herself a double espresso macchiato with extra whipped cream, because she deserved it. As she unwrapped a straw, she heard the bell chime and flinched at the memory of Reeve walking through the door right before she stole Patrick. She kept her head down, angrily stabbing her straw through the hole in the plastic lid, refusing to look until she heard Willow gasp. She glanced over at her boss to find her pale as a ghost and staring at the front door. Aster followed her gaze to find a giant of a man standing in the doorway.

He stood so tall, he had to duck to step inside. The man was dressed all in black: his jeans and T-shirt—even his hair was black. He tilted his head and sniffed the air before his dark eyes zeroed in on Aster and pinned her to the spot. The hair on the back of her neck stood up as he strode toward her, his leather boots thudding on the wooden floor, which vibrated under his weight. As he approached, she noticed his eyes flash amber briefly before returning to their normal brown. Both arms were covered in sleeve tattoos that ended at his wrists, drawing her attention to his hands clenched into fists and partially covered in tawny fur. He was on the verge of shifting, and that wouldn't be good for any human patrons to witness.

"Aster, danger," Willow whispered low enough for her hypersensitive hearing to pick up, and she prayed the man in black didn't hear it, too.

"Where is she?" the man growled when he came to a stop in front of Aster, forcing her to take a step backward, where her ass bumped into the counter.

"Where is who?" she asked, standing up straighter, refusing to be intimidated by the Neanderthal.

"Reeve. Where is she?"

"Who wants to know?" Aster cocked a hip, flipped her red hair over her shoulder, and crossed her arms over her chest.

"My name is Damian Stone, alpha of the Denver den, and Reeve is *my* mate." He leaned in closer, as if trying to make Aster bend over backwards, and she saw his canine teeth had grown into fangs. They bit into his bottom lip, drawing blood.

"Are you fucking kidding me?" She barked out a laugh, more like a maniacal cackle, as the anger toward her sister returned in full force. This was so typical. Reeve had left an alpha behind and was now shacked up with Patrick. Well, Reeve made the mess, so Reeve would have to clean it up. She ignored Willow's warning and said, "You can find her at Havenwood Village, Unit C. Two blocks that way." She pointed to the left, down Main Street.

Damian smirked and looked Aster up and down. "You're feisty. I like that. I might be back to add you to my collection. It won't be the first time I've had sisters." With that, he turned and stormed out of the coffee shop.

"Aster, what have you done?" Willow hissed. "That man is the big bad I've been sensing! He's emitting more crazy than a serial killer."

Aster's temper died out as quickly as it had flared, extinguished by Willow's statement. "I'm sorry!" She took a step to leave, to follow the man and stop him, when she was frozen in place.

"Don't even think about it, you stubborn ass," Harlow said as she approached with her hands raised like she was getting ready to catch a basketball. In between her palms, energy shimmered, clear yet tangible, like the surface of a lake. "You'll wind up getting hurt, too." Aster attempted to move again, but her friend's spell held strong.

Thankfully, only supes remained inside Coffee Haven, because Harlow could get in trouble for casting magic in public. "Let me go, Harlow," she demanded.

"Only if you agree to call your dad and let him know what's up. Willow is already calling the sheriff."

Aster stared at the front door long after Damian left. Willow's warning sank into her conscience, and worry turned her coffee sour in her stomach. *I just sent a dangerous, very large male I knew nothing about after Reeve*, she thought to herself. *What have I done?* She let out a cry when she envisioned Reeve, lifeless, in Damian's clutches.

"Okay, I promise!" The moment she said this, Harlow released the spell, and Aster almost fell over.

Without a word, Willow placed the coffee shop phone on the counter next to Aster's forgotten macchiato.

CHAPTER 4

*R*eeve woke up to Patrick lightly tracing a finger along her spine. She wiggled closer, forcing him to trail his finger down her side instead. When he hit the soft spot between her ribs and hip, she laughed. Realizing he had discovered a ticklish area, he tickled her even more, until she was breathless from laughing so hard. She'd forgotten what it was like to let her guard down and couldn't remember the last time she'd laughed like that. Then she remembered —it was before she met Damian Stone. Stone. His last name was appropriate, because she felt his weight like a boulder strapped to her back; just being in the same room as the alpha made it hard to breathe.

Thinking about Damian sobered her up, and she rolled away from Patrick, pulling the comforter over her naked body.

"Hey, what's wrong?" he asked, placing soft kisses on the top of her shoulder, which remained exposed. She knew she had to tell him about the situation she left behind in Denver and may have followed her to Havenwood Falls, but she struggled to form the words. "You can tell me anything. Whatever you're scared of, you have me now to protect you."

"What makes you think I'm scared?" she asked.

"We're bonded. I can feel what you're feeling."

"Right, I forgot about that part." Reeve closed her eyes and exhaled deeply before rolling over to face Patrick. His brown eyes were so different from Damian's. Where Damian's were hard and glinted like onyx, Patrick's were warm, like a dark honey. Yes, her mate swore to protect her, but Damian was a ruthless force. She placed a hand on Patrick's chest and ran her fingers through the coarse hair blanketing his pecs. His heart beat strong and steady under her palm.

"Talk to me, babe," he urged, placing a kiss on her forehead. "I bet you'll feel better after."

Reeve took a shaky breath and started from when she first met Damian Stone.

Denver, Late September

REEVE WAS WORKING for Elite Catering, which had been selected by the Denver mountain lion shifters for their Founders Day Celebration, a huge event that everyone in the shifter community anticipated each year. Since this past year was their twentieth annual party, the alpha wanted it to be special, so Reeve was brought in as the event planner. The party's venue was a warehouse that normally sat empty, providing a blank canvas every year for decorations and logistics.

When Reeve arrived at the warehouse for the first meeting, she met Damian Stone along with his beta, Gage Barrows, and Elite's executive chef. The meeting was typical—they went over the client's vision, timeline, and what to include on the menu. Reeve walked around the space, mapping out her ideas for decorations, table layout, and where to place the dance floor. The only thing atypical was Damian's behavior toward her. He came on strong and was relentless, despite her turning him down, citing Elite's non-fraternization policy prohibiting dating and personal relationships with current clients. Eventually, his beta got him to back off. Unfortunately, there were other meetings where Reeve didn't have anyone to run interference. She left those meetings disheveled from being pawed at. She asked her boss to remove her from the project, but there wasn't anyone else to take over. Reeve's boss asked her to stay on the job, and refuse Damian's advances as politely as possible. Then things really started to escalate.

Reeve had been casually dating a soldier with the Denver den. It was nothing serious—more like a friends with benefits situation—but when Damian found out, he ordered his soldier to stay away. Not too long after that, Reeve was at a club with some friends, having fun out on the dance floor. Reeve was dancing with some random guy, a human, and they started dancing pretty close. Her back was to his front, grinding to the beat, when suddenly he was gone. She turned around to see where he went, and Damian stood in his place. The poor human was sprawled out on the floor, unconscious, and by the way the bottom part of his jaw hung at an angle, she knew it was broken.

"You fucking psycho! What's wrong with you?" Reeve screamed in Damian's face. At this point, she'd had a couple of drinks and didn't think about the fact that Damian was a client. He had crossed a line, and she needed to push back.

"Nobody touches what's mine."

He said it with such arrogance that Reeve hauled off and slapped him, hoping to knock the smirk off his face. She didn't expect it to excite him, but he grabbed her by the hips, forcing her body against him.

Havenwood Falls

THE SOUND of Patrick growling caused Reeve to pause. His arm tightened around her from where it was draped across her side.

"Do you want me to stop?" she asked.

"I don't know. Did he…he hasn't raped you, has he?" He spat this question out like the very words choked him.

"No. No, never."

"Oh thank the gods!" he said with a deep exhale, and his body softened behind her.

Denver

NOBODY WAS ALLOWED to grab her like he did, like she was a piece of property, so she kneed him in the balls. By this time, they were creating quite the scene, and two of the club's bouncers arrived. When Damian's eyes started to glow, Reeve was afraid he would shift right there, but he managed to bring himself under control . . . barely. While the bouncers were busy with him, Reeve and her friends slipped out of the club.

The next day, her boss called and lit into Reeve about assaulting the company's number one client. Damian had twisted it all around, and made it seem like she was the one out of control—that she was the aggressor. Reeve gave her side of the story, and pleaded to be transferred to a different event, but Damian still insisted that Reeve be the event planner. Rather than be bullied and forced into a bad situation, she quit.

Two days later, her boss called, groveling. Reeve decided to go back to work not only because she loved her job, but because her boss agreed she would never have to be alone with Damian again. Her boss made sure Reeve had someone accompany her to any meeting or gathering. That worked for a few months, but Damian had a way of finding her outside of work. She'd run into him at Trader Joe's or at the coffee shop on the corner by her apartment. Fortunately, her building had security, and required a key card to get in; otherwise he probably would have shown up inside.

Havenwood Falls

REEVE SHIVERED at what she was about to tell Patrick. She'd been reliving the series of events over and over in her head since she fled Denver, and no one knew why she had returned to Havenwood Falls.

Patrick would be the first to hear about her situation, and it was only fair that she tell her mate. The bond compelled her to reveal everything —to bare her soul. There would be no secrets between them. She rolled over to face him, and he must have sensed her emotional distress because he tucked her close to his chest. She breathed in his scent, and noticing that hers mixed with his helped her to relax. Feeling better, she continued her story.

Denver

THE FOUNDERS DAY event celebrated the founding mountain lion shifters who established the den in Denver. They made it possible for other supes to move into the area, and helped build a strong community. Damian was really into family history and purity of bloodlines. Every time they had a meeting about the event, he made a point to talk about his heritage and how he's a direct descendent of Ransom Stone, the founding alpha. Reeve made the mistake of mentioning her father, and that he was an alpha. When Damian heard that, he certainly seemed to perk up, but Reeve had no idea just how obsessed he was in his belief that he needed to mate with the daughters of alphas, mating bond or not.

On the day of the Founders Day party, Reeve was busy working, attending to last minute details, and Damian was busy being host, so their paths never crossed, which was a relief to Reeve. After the party, only mountain lion shifters hung around. There was a nervous, pent-up energy in the warehouse that she recognized. The night was still young and the woods behind the warehouse beckoned. One of the Denver members asked if she wanted to shift and run with them.

"God yes," she exclaimed, relishing the perfect opportunity to unwind from a long, crazy day. On top of that, it had been at least two months since her last shift. Her skin itched with the need to let her cat out and play. So she filed out the back doors with the rest of the group, and they all stripped naked. Reeve's cat was anxious, and she shifted immediately then paced around the parking lot until everyone else had shifted.

Damian's cat was easy to spot. He was the biggest, with a square, masculine face. The dark markings around his eyes and nose looked like war paint, and added to his fierce intensity. His amber eyes locked on Reeve's before he bounded off across a small field that separated the warehouse from the trees. The warehouse was located on the border of the Rocky Mountain Arsenal National Wildlife Refuge, and provided the perfect cover for shifters. Mountain lion sightings weren't unusual and never drew much attention. The rest of the shifters followed suit, and soon Reeve was running in the wilderness, the city lights of Denver just a distant, hazy glow on the horizon.

They ran for the thickest section of the forest, to minimize the risk of crossing paths with humans. With the wind ruffling through her fur and a hint of summer in the warm night air, Reeve let the stress of the past few weeks melt away. The more she ran and her paws connected with the soft earth, the more the human part of her let go—it was such a release. She was so caught up in the moment that she didn't realize she had split off from the group and run into an unfamiliar area. She sniffed the air and surrounding trees, brushes, and rocks for any familiar scents, but didn't detect anything. She came across a stream and crouched down for a drink. The entire time her ears were at attention, twitching at every noise. In the distance she heard the cry of prey expelling its last breath. Reeve lifted her head from the cold water and looked in the direction of the hunt. Moments later, a faint trace of blood clung to the wind, and her nostrils flared with interest. Scenting her kind, she started heading in that direction.

By the time she arrived, traces of the fresh kill were all that remained. Tufts of gray rabbit fur floated in the air, while some clumps were glued to the earth with blood and guts. Multiple paw prints in the mud showed that more than one mountain lion had passed through. Reeve was also back in familiar territory. The night sky was fading into dawn when she arrived back at the warehouse, and she immediately noticed something was amiss.

Her dress and heels, which she had left in a neat pile by the door, were missing. She quickly shifted, and the moment she felt her bones pop into the right place, she stood up straight from where she was crouched. Figuring someone had mistakenly moved them, she went inside to look. There she did find them—in Damian's hands. Reeve didn't sense anyone else in the building. They were alone in the dimly lit space, and she immediately went on the defensive.

"Why do you have my clothes?" she asked, and held her arm out in a silent demand for their return. Her other arm was pressed across her breasts, where Damian's gaze had been fixed since she walked in.

"Because you're mine, and I can do what I want."

"Oh, for fuck's sake! How many times do I have to tell you? I am not yours. Now give me my damn clothes."

Reeve made it a point to stay in one place and not move toward him. He could come to her, and she had the exit at her back in case he tried anything stupid. His dark eyes glinted in the faint light, and his smirk turned into a wide grin full of sharp teeth. His canines lengthened, and he took a step closer. Reeve tensed and resisted taking a step back, not wanting him to see that she was intimidated. Instead she stood up taller and adjusted her long hair so it covered her breasts. Her arms appeared relaxed at her sides, but she was ready to fight if it came to that. Reeve didn't know Damian very well, but she'd been around him enough to know he was drunk on his power, and he struggled to keep control of his beast. The display of teeth just confirmed it for her.

"You definitely have alpha blood flowing through your veins. So proud and defiant, but you will submit to me," he said.

"No. I won't," she replied, never taking her eyes off him. Damian took another step toward her. He was stalking his prey, and she prepared to spring backwards. Her toes sought out some sort of purchase on the concrete.

He handed Reeve her dress, and she flinched at first, which made him chuckle. Glaring at him, she reached for the thin silk and fell right into his trap. As soon as she had the dress in her hand, he snatched her wrist and yanked her toward him, crushing her against his chest. She started to resist, and at first didn't register the sting in her left butt cheek. The fucker had a syringe full of sedative, and Reeve's ability to fight evaporated. She still tried, even though her arms and legs felt like they were made of lead.

WHEN SHE CAME TO, Reeve was in a small bedroom, lying on a single bed. Sunlight streamed in through the only window. It took her a few minutes to shake the grogginess off. Her eyelids felt weighed down, but Reeve wasn't about to go back under, so she forced herself to sit up, and the room spun. Finally, the dizzy spell passed, and she swung her legs over the side of the bed. Her feet making contact with cold tiles provided enough of a jolt to wake her up fully. She took stock of her situation and realized someone had dressed her—at least partially—while she was unconscious. She was wearing a large Harley Davidson T-shirt that fit more like a dress, it was so big. It also carried a scent she was becoming too familiar with—Damian's. There was a sour smell underneath the male musk that repelled her. Her inner cat had zero interest in his pheromones—they were definitely not a match.

Reeve wanted so badly to rip the shirt off, but she left it on to avoid being naked and more vulnerable. She did a quick inventory of her body to see if anything was wrong. Anything could have happened while she was unconscious, but fortunately, she found she wasn't injured and didn't have any tenderness to indicate she had been raped. She slowly rose to her feet, anticipating another round of dizziness that didn't come. There was a bottle of water on the floor next to the bed, and she drained it in seconds. Whatever Damian had drugged her with had left her with severe cottonmouth.

It didn't take her long to check the bedroom for weapons or a way out. The door was locked, and the window had bars on it. The closet was empty, and the bed was just a mattress on a frame, so there weren't any bedposts to snap off and use as a weapon. Reeve peered out the window to get an idea of where she was being held. She was on the second floor and had a view of a nondescript backyard that was surrounded by tall oak trees blocking the view of anything beyond.

Sitting on the windowsill in the sunshine, she closed her eyes and listened to her surroundings.

Through the wall to her right, she heard soft whimpers like a woman crying, and to the left, someone was pacing. A male voice could be heard on the first floor. It was muffled and hard to tell whether it belonged to Damian or one of his men, or if it was just a TV show. A second male voice joined in, and the muffled conversation that followed was interrupted by what sounded like plates clanging against each other. None of this information helped Reeve, so she sat back down on the bed to think. If she was only asleep for a few hours, then it was Saturday. If she didn't show up for work on Monday, someone would come to look for her. She was last seen at the party, but she could have been in another county for all she knew. She didn't have her bag, phone, or car, since they were probably left at the warehouse.

As she sat there, more noises came from downstairs, as well as the smell of food. Her stomach growled when she caught a whiff of bacon. Minutes later, footsteps approached, and they stopped nearby. She heard a door open and close. Not long after that, the same door opened and closed, a squeak of the hinges its tell. Then the footsteps stopped outside of the room Reeve was being held in, and she waited with uneasy anticipation as a key slid into the lock and the knob turned. Reflexively, she assumed a defensive crouched position on top of the bed. A guy about her sister's age came into the room carrying a tray of food.

"Scott, right?" she asked, recognizing him as one of the den's soldiers from the party.

He didn't acknowledge her at all, or even look at her. He placed the tray on the floor by the bed and backed out of the room. It only took a few seconds.

"Wait—come back!" she yelled. His retreating footsteps paused in what she assumed was a hallway. "I need to use the bathroom." This wasn't a lie. She really did have to go, but she also wanted an opportunity to learn more about where she was being held, such as the layout and exit points.

Scott came back. He stood in the doorway and held up a pair of handcuffs. "You're not leaving the room until you put these on," he said, still not meeting her eyes. He was at least six feet tall and had a muscular build like Reeve's brother, Braden. While he wasn't making eye contact, Scott was tracking her every move. He didn't have to worry. She wasn't going to challenge him—at least not yet.

Reeve approached him with her arms held out, and he handcuffed her. Then he pulled out a gun from the back of his black cargo pants, and she gasped.

"Relax, it's a tranq gun. If you behave, I won't use it. Now, let's go." He nudged her forward with the muzzle of the gun, and they stepped out into a long hallway. There were three other doors on the right side, in addition to her room, and two doors on the left. At the end of the hallway, Reeve noticed a flight of stairs leading down. They walked until they reached the door on the left closest to the stairs.

"Here you go," Scott pushed open the door to reveal a bathroom.

Reeve went inside, relieved when he didn't follow. She closed the door and went to lock it, but there wasn't a lock available. Quickly scanning the room, Reeve was hit with disappointment again when she realized there weren't any windows. She did her business and checked the medicine cabinet for anything useful, but only found cotton swabs, a box of tampons, and a tube of toothpaste. Closing the cabinet, she caught a glimpse of her reflection in the mirror. Her hair was a tangled mess, and smudges of dirt made her right cheek look bruised. Using hand soap, she washed her face and scrubbed the makeup off from the night before. The handcuffs made it challenging, but she worked around them. Unable to stall anymore, she took a deep breath and opened the door. Scott was waiting across the hall, leaning against the wall, which was painted a light dove gray and accented with white wainscoting. Wherever they were keeping her, it had been recently decorated.

Scott herded her back to "her" room, removed the handcuffs, and left without a word. Reeve sat down on the bed and eyed the tray of food. A pile of scrambled eggs and bacon were on a paper plate, and there was a paper bowl of mixed berries on the side along with a cup of orange juice and a cup of coffee. Propped up against the glass of juice was an envelope with her name on it. Curiosity got the best of her, so she grabbed it and set the tray aside on the bed. There was a single sheet of paper inside with a handwritten note from Damian.

Reeve,

You probably think of me as some monster, but I'm not doing this for me. This is for our race. I do this to ensure our future. Our alpha blood will make our offspring stronger and faster. We've become too diluted, especially since inter-shifter marriages became legal.

Someday you will grow to appreciate what I'm building here, and perhaps even develop feelings for me. I can give you a good life as your provider, and we can create a generation of pure-blooded cats to help sustain our kind. You're strong and fierce, qualities I seek in a mate. It pains me to have to keep you locked up, but until I can trust you, this is how things have to be. I hope you choose to behave and accept your fate.

Your Mate and Alpha,

Damian

Reeve's appetite vanished after reading his note. She'd heard of species purists, but never met one. Supes weren't any different than humans. There were some who were progressive, others who were conservative, and then there were those who were resistant to change no matter what. Reeve was glad the national leadership for shifters legalized inter-species marriage, recognizing the need to align with human legislation.

Fortunately, Denver was progressive. Well, except for Damian. What struck Reeve as weird was that there weren't any warnings about Damian, so either he didn't have a lot of support in Denver, or his supporters knew how to fly under the radar. Reeve knew she was not going to be his mate, and certainly not a breeding whore. He was out of his ever-loving mind if he thought he'd control her. His note did confirm that she was dealing with a different kind of crazy, and from that point forward she needed to do everything within her power to be at one hundred percent.

Despite her loss of appetite, and while the food and coffee were lukewarm, Reeve consumed everything. She didn't smell anything off, so it hadn't been tainted, and she needed to eat to keep her strength up. Reading his note again turned the rock in her stomach into a ball of rage. Who did this asshole think he was? And Reeve already had an alpha—her dad. Even though she had left Havenwood Falls, she never swore a loyalty oath to another den.

When you're alone without anything to occupy your time except for your thoughts, it's a good time for reflection. Aside from a few friends from school and work, Reeve didn't have a huge social network in Denver—even though she'd lived there for more than six years. She'd always planned to eventually come home and be with her family and the den. She didn't realize how homesick she really was, and soon came to the realization that it could be days until someone noticed she was missing.

Havenwood Falls

REEVE PAUSED to catch her breath. Now that she was able to talk about her experience and personal revelations, the words poured out. The fact that Patrick listened without interruption was nice, too. He had stopped pacing the room and joined her in bed again. Occasional kisses on her neck and shoulders or a reassuring squeeze gave her encouragement to continue. It was hard to believe that just three days before they were total strangers yet she never felt so connected to anyone. The connection came from deep within and was more than physical, although they had spent most of the weekend in bed with the exception of eating and showering.

Reeve traced a finger along Patrick's chest and up his neck, the smooth skin transitioning to rough stubble when she approached his jawline. Her fingertip came to a rest on the dimple in his chin and she watched as the corners of his mouth lifted into a grin.

"Finish your story, love. We can play later," he whispered, lifting her finger to his lips and kissing the tip before placing her hand on his hip.

"Deal," she said with a sigh and snuggled against him. "First, I have to explain that I left Havenwood Falls for Aster. You're new to town, so you don't know how miserable Aster was being my younger sister." Reeve sighed. "I hated that she was miserable, and it wasn't as if I *tried* to be popular. I'm fairly outgoing, and in middle school and high school, people just gravitated towards me." She shrugged. "Classes were easy for me, too, so I succeeded as a student. But Aster was shy, and school was harder for her. When I tried to help, she thought I was taking pity on her. It didn't help that, with us being two years apart, she was constantly being compared to me." Reeved paused for a breath and rearranged herself before continuing. "It wasn't fair to hold myself back, and our parents were concerned that I would—and they were right. I love Aster and would do anything for her. So I thought it best to leave Havenwood Falls and began applying to colleges. My parents heard me out and were concerned about Aster, too. Braden, our big brother, was always running interference and trying to maintain peace between us. He even agreed with my plan. So, my parents made arrangements for me to leave. I'm not sure what my dad had to do in order to get approval from the Court to have a spell put on me to counteract the memory spell. He has never told me. Less than a year later, I left for Denver."

"You did that for Aster?" Patrick asked, and she heard the awe in his voice.

"Well, yeah, she's my sister. It worked too. She was able to grow up as Aster McCabe, not Reeve McCabe's little sister."

"I had no idea. Aster alluded to a rivalry of sorts, but she never went into detail."

"She wouldn't as it wasn't a good period for us. We definitely had our moments and defined cat fights," Reeve joked, earning a chuckle from Patrick that rumbled deep in his chest like a purr. It lightened the tension Reeve felt building like a storm inside her, but that was short lived. She still had to finish telling Patrick about Damian.

"So, anyway, I was reflecting on my life and what led me to being held prisoner by a whack job I swore that if I was lucky enough to escape Damian, that I'd return home and start working on my relationship with Aster. I mean, we're both adults now, and hopefully enough time has passed to heal any old wounds. I latched onto this goal like a drowning person holding onto a lifesaver, and it made me more determined than ever to find a way out."

"And then you come home and meet me. Fuck! Aster has to be hurting so bad right now. We were supposed to be going away this weekend for our six-month anniversary." Patrick was out of bed again and pacing his room. He ran his hands through his hair, which already stood up in spikes because right after his last shower, they had found their way back in bed. At this point, his hair looked like it had been through a hurricane.

"I know." Reeve struggled to swallow, her throat suddenly thick with emotion. "We can't control who our mate is, though. This is something Damian Stone doesn't understand." Thinking of the man replaced the sadness with anger. She'd been through hell for months because of that asshole.

"How did you get away from him?" Patrick asked.

Reeve returned to her story.

Somewhere Near Denver

SCOTT CAME BACK to check on her a few hours later, and after handcuffing her again, escorted her to the bathroom. She hadn't showered, and was still just wearing Damian's T-shirt. She wasn't concerned about showing skin, but didn't like feeling vulnerable. She asked Scott if she could get some real clothes, and he said he'd check with Damian. Then he locked her back up in the room again. Shadows grew longer as the day wore on, and Reeve paced the room until her legs ached. She curled up on the bed, facing the door, and stared at the doorknob as if willing it to turn. At some point she fell asleep, because she woke up with Damian curled up behind her, one of his hands on her bare thigh.

Screaming, Reeve leapt off the bed and landed on all fours in a crouch. Her entire body shuddered, on the verge of shifting, but she fought back the urge. A muffled growl came from the room next door, and something hit against the other side of the wall.

"Now is that any way to greet your mate?" Damian said. He remained lying on the bed, shirtless, but Reeve thanked God he still had jeans on. Under different circumstances, she'd probably find him attractive. He was a solid male specimen, of that there was no doubt, but his size just made her realize how much smaller she was in comparison.

Reeve didn't respond to his question and remained silent, glaring at him from her crouched position.

He clucked his tongue at her like she was an errant child, and slithered off the bed. He probably thought he was being sexy and seductive, but his movements were predatory. Reeve warily watched him approach and didn't back away. He came to stand in front of her and squatted down so they were eye to eye. "Such gorgeous green eyes. I hope at least one of our children inherits those."

Reeve flinched, and he seemed to enjoy this momentary lapse in her façade.

"Scott tells me you requested clothes?"

He caught her off guard with the change of subject. She nodded.

"You can have clothes and a shower, but only with one condition."

This shouldn't have surprised her. He had all of the negotiating power at this point. "What's that?"

"You have to eat dinner with me. We should get to know each other. We'll eat downstairs since you've been cooped up in here all day. Do you accept?"

The idea of seeing more of the house was the hook that made her say yes. Damian, pleased with her answer, stood to go, and she slowly rose out of the crouched position.

"See you in one hour," he said, before leaving the room. Seconds later, she heard the key turn in the lock.

True to his word, Damian sent Scott a few minutes later with a pair of black lace panties and a bra. He handed Reeve a little black cocktail dress and set a pair of red heels on the floor. Apparently dinner was going to be a formal affair. He escorted Reeve to the bathroom again, where towels were laid out for her and a plush cotton robe hung on a hook by the shower. A toothbrush and toothpaste had also appeared. They were on the edge of the sink next to a wide-toothed comb.

Reeve took her time in the shower, hoping the warm water would relax her muscles, but they might as well have been made of concrete, she was so tense about the dinner. Based on the sexy, lacy underthings, she suspected Damian had her in mind for dessert. That was not happening. A knock on the door told Reeve her time was up. With a sigh, she turned off the faucets.

Damian appeared at the door to her room with a bouquet of red roses in hand. It was like he thought he was showing up at her apartment to take her on a date—not that she was his prisoner and had zero choice in the matter. Scott followed him into the room carrying a plastic vase of water, which he placed on the windowsill. "No glass until we establish some trust," Damian explained as he set the roses in the vase.

They left the room, Damian cupping Reeve's elbow and keeping her close to his side, while Scott picked up the rear. As they walked down the hallway, they passed the door for the room next to Reeve's, the room where she had heard someone growl earlier.

"That's Phoebe's room. She's a willful one, too. It must be a trait with alpha females. She misbehaved earlier; otherwise she'd be joining us for dinner."

Reeve's stomach sank when he confirmed that another shifter was being held captive. If she had needed confirmation this guy wasn't hooked up right, that would have been it, but she already knew he wasn't playing with a full deck.

"What did she do?" Reeve asked, curiosity getting the best of her.

"She tried to kill herself by slicing her wrists with her claws."

Jesus! Reeve thought. She would have had to partially shift to make that happen. Suicide among shifters was rare to almost nonexistent. It was as if they were wired for survival no matter what.

"Tamara is on the other side of you, but she's moving tonight to my house, as she finally submitted. She earned my trust, and soon we'll have a mating ceremony."

"This isn't your house?" Reeve asked.

"Well, I own it, but I don't live here. This is more of a training facility, and only a select few know its true purpose."

They reached the top of the stairs, and Damian guided Reeve forward with his hand on the small of her back. The heat radiating off his skin burned through the thin fabric of her dress, and she imagined a handprint forever imprinted on her back like a brand. For the first time, she was being taken downstairs. At the bottom, to the right, was the front door, and her heart raced at the close proximity, until she noticed the three different locks, all requiring a key. Directly across the hall, there was a sparsely furnished living room. The furniture looked stiff and uncomfortable, more for decoration than function, like a setup in a model home. Damian steered Reeve to the left, away from the front door, and down a short hallway into a dining room. The chandelier over the table cast dim lighting, and the table was set for two, with another bouquet of roses and two white taper candles as the centerpiece.

Damian held a chair out for her, and she sank down on the cushion, the straight back forcing her to sit just as straight. An older woman appeared through a side door and poured red wine into their glasses. She kept her eyes down in deference to Damian. Her gray hair was pulled back into a bun, making her entire weather-beaten face visible.

"Dinner will be served in ten minutes, sir," she said, looking at the floor.

"Good. Right on schedule. Thank you, Marta," Damian responded, dismissing her with a nod. The woman left as silently as she arrived, and Damian lifted his glass into the air for a toast. "To the future of our kind, and that our children grow up to be a generation of strong leaders."

He held his glass out toward her, but Reeve refused to pick up hers. Like hell was she going to toast to that.

"Come on now, Reeve. We can do this the easy way or the hard way."

"Great. The easy way is to let me go." She stood up and started walking to the front of the house. Damian thundered behind her, and suddenly his arms were around her waist. Before she could react, he picked her up and carried her back into the dining room, where he forcefully placed her in the chair.

"You are not leaving. The sooner you get that through that stubborn brain of yours, the easier it will be for you. Unless you prefer being locked up in that tiny room?"

Reeve didn't say anything, but glared at him and couldn't control her lip from curling up as a growl rumbled deep in her chest. Her cat begged to be set free, the idea of captivity just as unappealing to her as it was to Reeve. They sometimes disagreed on things, but on this they were in full accord. Damian was dangerous and a threat to their independence, to their future. Reeve thought of Phoebe, the other alpha female who was a stranger to her, but her sister in this experience. She was desperate enough to attempt suicide, and Reeve refused to get to that point. Now wasn't the time to fight, and as hard as it was to do, she called to her cat and coaxed her down. *Soon*, Reeve promised her cat.

❧

Havenwood Falls

"Jesus fucking Christ. This guy has more captives? What the fuck? I'm going to find him and end his ass. He's fucking done!" Patrick raged and punched the wall next to the door, leaving a fist-sized hole in the drywall.

"No!" Reeve cried out and reached for his hand, pulling him back to bed. He reluctantly sat down on the edge, but his back was ramrod straight, the muscles in his shoulders tensed for a fight. "He's lethal. It's too dangerous! But," she paused.

"But what?" He turned to look at her.

"What if he follows me here? I think he's crazy enough to do it."

"Good." Patrick stood and turned to face her, his entire naked body on display; every cord of muscle there for her to see. His eyes had turned the color of molten gold and blazed with fury. He was shorter than Damian, but only by a couple of inches and equally built. "Let him come here. He's a fool if he does. I'll die protecting you and so will your den."

"You don't understand. The last conversation I had with Damian scared the shit out of me…and my cat."

"What did he say?"

~

Somewhere Near Denver

REEVE RESOLVED to shut Damian out, and ate in complete silence. Right before he locked her up in her room that night, she broke down and asked him one question. "Is your entire den on board with this plan of yours?"

He grinned, a display of strong, sharp teeth. "Not everyone knows of the plan, and I've been challenged a few times, but I'm still here and the challengers . . . well, they're dead."

On that chilling note, he closed the door. The sound of the lock being engaged seemed to echo in Reeve's ears, putting her inner cat on full alert.

She didn't sleep that night. Instead she perched on the windowsill, staring at the stars and getting her bearings. The window faced west, and a faint glow in the distance told Reeve there was some sort of city, town, hell, even an airport or something nearby that emitted a lot of light. She hoped it was Denver, but even if it wasn't, that glow was a beacon in the darkness. If she could get out of the house, she'd make a break for it, because she was light on her paws and had always been one of the fastest runners in the den. She mentally reviewed the layout of the house over and over again, trying to recall the smallest of details that might mean a way out of captivity. Then finally it dawned on her how she could escape. She couldn't be handcuffed, though. The cuffs prevented her from shifting.

The sky was beginning to lighten by the time Reese formulated her plan. With her mind at ease, she crawled into bed and fell asleep. This time when she woke up, Damian wasn't in bed with her, and she didn't hear any movement on the second floor. A tray of breakfast food was on the floor by the bed. Knowing she needed the energy to shift, she ate everything. Not too long after that, she heard someone coming up the stairs. Based on the heaviness of the tread, she could tell it was a man. Crouching down by the floor, she pressed her nose near the gap underneath the door and inhaled. She recognized the scent and smiled, since she had factored Scott into her plan. She quickly stood up and quietly moved to stand behind the door.

Just as she planned, it swung open, and when Scott didn't see her, he stepped farther into the room and made the mistake of not looking behind the door first. He had the handcuffs in one hand, which left him at yet another disadvantage. It only took her seconds to shift, and Reeve didn't even wait for all four paws to hit the ground before she pounced. He turned toward her, and she bowled him over onto his back. In one fluid motion, she locked her jaws over his throat, and hot blood burst into her mouth as she ripped his throat out. His heart stuttered once before it grew silent forever.

She didn't linger, but bounded down the hall, practically leaping down the stairs with one jump. She slid a little bit on the hardwood floor when she landed and struggled to gain traction, but it didn't matter. Her presence was still undetected. She darted down the short hallway and into the dining room, where the exit had been behind her back the entire time she was eating dinner. French doors led out to a patio. These doors didn't have bars covering the panes of glass, which shattered and rained down in a million glittering pieces when she smashed through them. The backyard was empty, but Reeve heard voices shouting behind her. They spurred her cat into action. With the lingering taste of copper on her tongue from Scott's blood, she disappeared into the woods and kept running.

Havenwood Falls

"THAT'S HOW I ESCAPED, and once I did, I ran in the direction of the hazy glow and found my way to the outskirts of Denver, not far from the warehouse. Not surprisingly, my car was gone from the parking lot. I didn't want to risk going into Denver and seeing my friends. I mean, that's the first place Damian would look for me, right?"

Patrick murmured in agreement, but didn't say anything. She coaxed him back into bed, hoping to calm him down. He rejoined her and wrapped his arms around her, but he was so tense, she might as well have been in the arms of a marble statue. She tilted her head to look at him and noticed his eyes glowing. The human pupils were replaced by catlike slits. Reeve could feel his anger as if it was her own. She was still not used to the bond, so it was a little overwhelming.

"Hey, I'm okay. I'm here. I stayed in the woods and in my cat form until I reached Havenwood Falls. I arrived at my parents' back door late Thursday night. They were surprised to see me standing naked on the deck, and they had a lot of questions, but I was too exhausted to answer them."

"Does your dad know about this Damian guy?" Patrick asked, his cat eyes boring into Reeve's.

"No. My dad was in a meeting when I woke up, and my mom was gone, so I headed right down to Coffee Haven to see Aster."

"And then you met me."

"And then I met you . . . and we've been in bed ever since," Reeve said with a mischievous grin, and wiggled against Patrick, getting the desired reaction.

He grinned back, and his eyes returned to normal as he rolled over so he was on top of Reeve and her legs were wrapped around his hips.

Patrick was about ready to enter her when a loud boom shook the walls. He practically flew off her, almost as if he was levitating, and he shifted midair before landing in a crouch on the floor, positioning himself between the door and the bed, ready to protect his mate.

"Oh, shit!" Reeve shouted when the bedroom door crashed open and she saw Damian standing in the doorway.

The crazy fucker had actually followed her to her hometown, onto her territory.

She watched with dread as Damian shifted, and Patrick went on the attack. The snarling, clawing mass of fur moved out of the bedroom and into the hallway. Patrick immediately dominated and forced Damian back toward the broken front door. Reeve couldn't believe it, because Damian was clearly one of the largest cats she had ever seen, but Patrick was faster and delivering more swipes. His claws dug deep into Damian's side, and blood immediately welled up, but Damian didn't even flinch.

The fight moved into the living room, escalating with each assault. Blood sprayed onto walls, and bloody paw prints covered the floor. Patrick moved in for another swipe, but Damian pivoted at the last minute, pouncing onto Patrick's back. Teeth and claws sunk in deep, and when Patrick yelped, Reeve's heart almost stopped beating. The instinct to protect her mate took over, and she dropped the bed sheet she had wrapped around her body to shift. The moment she was completely transformed, she launched at Damian, tackling him from the side and dislodging his grip from Patrick. She hit him with such force that they rolled out of the hole where the front door used to be, and down two stairs onto the front walkway.

Damian growled and hissed as they circled each other on the small lawn. Reeve kept crouched low, her gaze unwavering until movement behind Damian caught her attention. Patrick stalked down the small set of stairs to join the fray. She noticed he favored his right rear leg, which was shredded, the exposed muscle and tissue red and raw against his sandy brown fur. That momentary distraction gave Damian a window, and he seized the opportunity, knocking Reeve over and pinning her on her back. He was much heavier and more solid than her brother Braden, whom she used to spar with, and she knew she was outmatched, but she wasn't going to give up.

Damian snapped his jaws near her face, trying to access her throat, but she evaded him. Using her hind legs, she scratched at his soft underbelly, and when he wavered, this provided the encouragement she needed. Lodging her legs under him, she pushed with all of her strength and succeeded in shoving him off while deepening the wounds on his stomach.

Patrick leaped over Reeve, where she was still lying prone on the ground, and went on the attack again. At this point, they had drawn a crowd. Patrick's neighbors in the surrounding apartments stepped out onto their front steps, a gathering of werewolves, witches, fae, and humans. Reeve heard sirens in the distance, and she knew the sheriff and a containment team had been dispatched. A sharp crack followed by a loud yelp sent Patrick to the ground. Shattered bone stuck out through the wound on his previously injured leg. Damian moved in for the kill.

CHAPTER 5

*A*ster snatched up the phone and called her dad. He answered immediately.

"Aster, what is it? I'm in the middle of something." He sounded breathless, which was highly unusual. Her dad was more in shape than someone half his age.

"Dad, I think I screwed up and put Reeve in danger." He paused on the other end and grew eerily quiet.

"What did you do?" he asked.

Aster hesitated and glanced over at Willow, who was standing behind the counter listening. She nodded in encouragement, so Aster took a deep breath before spilling the story out. He didn't even wait for her to finish, but he got the gist.

"Damn it, Aster. She's your sister, not your enemy. If you only knew what she sacrificed for you."

Aster pictured her dad pinching the bridge of his nose, something he always did when he was agitated with her. "You need to stay put at the shop. There's no need for you getting in the middle. I've heard whispers about this guy and he's not playing with a full deck."

"Okay, but I want to help, Dad. I didn't know this guy was such bad news."

"Just stay there. At least I know you're safe and won't have to worry about you, too." He hung up the phone.

"What did he say?" Willow asked. She had come out from behind the counter and sat down at the table with Aster.

"He wants me to stay here."

Just then a sheriff's patrol car screamed by the coffee shop, its blue lights flashing. A second patrol car followed right behind it. They headed in the direction of Patrick's place.

"Shit," she said out loud and stood up quickly, almost knocking her chair over.

"Wait!" Willow reached out and grabbed hold of Aster's hand. "You need to stay here."

Aster reluctantly sat down again, but she was restless and literally sat on the edge of her seat, her gaze not wavering from the front picture window. Minutes ticked by slowly on the wall clock behind the counter. Her sensitive hearing attuned to the steady tick, tick, tick as time marched forward. Cell phones erupted all around her as notifications and ringtones went off. She caught snippets of whispered conversations about a fight up the street between mountain lions. That's all she needed to hear. She stood up, this time knocking her chair over.

"Aster!" Willow called after her, but she was out the door and running up the street before Harlow had the chance to cast another spell. She ran past the bookstore, and other businesses flashed by in a blur as she deftly dodged pedestrians who were in her way. An ambulance raced past, its sirens hurting her ears. Up ahead, she saw a collection of flashing lights. A patrol car was parked across Main Street, blocking traffic.

Aster slipped through an opening in a hedge and ran across several lawns to reach the front of Patrick's development, where all of the action seemed to be concentrated. She came to a sudden stop when she saw her brother, Braden, locked in a fight with the largest mountain lion she'd ever seen. She recognized her brother's markings; the tops of his ears were tipped with black fur, and he had a unique diamond-shaped patch of white right above his nose. The rest of his fur was dark and matted with blood. Fresh wounds oozed from both sides of his body.

Then Aster took in the rest of the scene unfolding in front of her. Patrick lay on the grass, off to the side like a discarded piece of trash. Reeve kneeled beside him, holding his hand as a medic treated his wounds. She wore a bathrobe that had been loosely cinched at her waist. Patrick had a surgical green sheet draped over the lower half of his body. Aster suspected they had both fought in their cat forms, leaving them naked as the day they were born when they shifted back.

Braden, distracted by Aster's appearance on the sidelines, turned his head to hiss at her, and Damian attacked. His jaws clamped down on Braden's neck, and the ensuing snap was deafening. Braden went limp, and his eyes focused on some distant point before she saw the light fade.

"No!" she shrieked, and her inner cat rose to the surface, ready and anxious to join the fight to avenge her brother's death.

Reeve's cry joined hers when to their horror, their father stepped onto the bloodied lawn. His cat bore the scars of previous battles: a clipped ear, healed-over claw marks where scar tissue prevented fur from growing. He was battle-worn, but each scar told a story of survival. He was the alpha of their den for a reason.

Sheriff's deputies circled the fight to prevent anyone else from joining the fray. Sheriff Kasun had his tranquilizer gun trained on Damian, but he didn't fire. This was an alpha versus alpha confrontation now, and the sheriff, alpha of the Havenwood Falls wolf pack, respected the significance. Aster's heart pounded in her throat, and tears spilled freely as she moved her way through the gathering crowd to reach her fallen brother. People stepped aside to let her pass, clearing a path. Jordan, an EMT and one of Braden's friends who had grown up in their family's den, was trying his best to resuscitate, but Braden had shifted back to his human form, and his skin was already taking on a gray pallor. She sunk down to her knees on the other side of him and took her brother's hand. This was her fault. She sent that monster to Reeve, she put her sister in danger, and Braden had paid the ultimate price defending their family. Braden's hand was growing cold in hers, as if she was drawing all of the warmth out.

"I'm sorry, Aster. He's gone," Jordan whispered the words she dreaded to hear.

"No! No!" she cried out. Leaning forward, she crouched over her brother and placed her head on his chest. The sounds of the fight were drowned out as grief consumed her, yet a strange thrumming in her blood prevented her from disconnecting completely.

Her cat grew restless as if she paced underneath Aster's skin, wanting to break free, her attention focused on something approaching. Aster's sobs stilled as she concentrated on the presence drawing closer. She sniffed the air as the most tantalizing and alluring scent she had ever detected grew stronger. Her blood thrummed deep inside, and her heart beat faster. She heard footsteps coming up behind her, causing her to raise her head from her brother's chest and look.

A man stood not even five feet away. His eyes were a dark blue, like the color of the river when it reflected the sky on a clear day. He was tall and broad; his shirt barely contained the muscles straining beneath. His sandy blond hair stuck up in some areas, like he had just woken up. Her cat purred in appreciation and urged Aster to her feet. She felt inexplicably drawn to this stranger, and his nostrils flared as she approached, his eyes flashing amber briefly. Then he held his hand out to her. The moment they touched, a shock reverberated through her, like the earth shifted under her feet. Aster gasped and gripped the man's hand tighter, and she realized she never wanted to let go. He was her anchor. She felt it in her soul, and her cat did, too.

"Mate?" he asked, his eyebrows rising in shock.

"I think so," she said, breathless. "I'm Aster."

"Gage Barrows." His deep voice sent shivers down her spine, and she moved closer. Gage responded by circling her in his strong arms. She nuzzled his chest, absorbing his scent and marking him with hers. He was her mate. At this confirmation, a deep sense of contentment and belonging settled something that she hadn't realized needed settling. "What happened, Aster? I sense your pain."

The world came crashing back, her brief suspension from reality ending with his question. Shame washed over her again. Braden was dead and lying feet away, and she had already forgotten about him. *Was she always so selfish?*

"Hey, talk to me," Gage pleaded. He tilted her head up so she had to meet his eyes. She blinked fresh tears away and swallowed past the lump in her throat.

"My brother is dead. That bastard killed him." She pointed in the direction of the fight and sensed Gage tense.

"Shit! That bastard is my alpha," he growled and narrowed his eyes as he watched the bloody brawl.

"Well, he's fighting my father now, and he's my alpha." They both tensed and gripped each other's hands tight.

Aster noticed her father slowing down, and she cried out when Damian swiped at him, causing her father to stumble backwards and lose his footing.

"Not my father, too! This is my mess, and I need to fix it," she told Gage and stepped away from her mate.

Her cat whimpered at the separation. Aster ignored the urge to touch him and called her cat forward. Her muscles snapped and bones popped as she shifted into her cat form. The assault on her senses overwhelmed her at first. The metallic tang of blood that hung in the air was so much stronger, and the multiple heartbeats pulsing around her sounded like a circle of drums. Her mate's scent dominated her senses, though, and she wanted to slink around his legs and rub against him, but then she heard her father grunt as he suffered another blow.

Barreling past bystanders who cried out in surprise, she rushed the deputy who had his back to her, focused on the fight and not the threat creeping up behind him. She sprung, knocking him down, and ran past him into the fight. Damian had his back end to her, too, his focus on her father, who was uncharacteristically retreating and unable to put pressure on his front left leg. Aster charged and attempted to knock Damian over so his underbelly would be exposed, but her impact jarred her more than him, and she bounced off like a ball against a brick wall. Damian turned to face her and he grinned, revealing a mouth full of vicious teeth stained red with the blood of her family.

Aster shook off the impact and crouched down, her claws digging into the soil for traction. She hissed at the monster in front of her, goading him. Let him spring first, and then she'd slice him open once he was in the air and his belly exposed. Damian's grin faltered, and he hissed back. *Could he read her mind?* Then she noticed the crowd had quieted, reminding her of the eerie stillness before a storm erupts.

Just then, another mountain lion entered the fight. She'd never seen this cat before, but she recognized his scent—her mate. Gage moved to stand between Aster and Damian, his backside to Aster so she knew he joined in her defense. His tail flicked with agitation, and his ears were flattened as if pinned to his head. He was equal in size to Damian and absolutely beautiful. His coat glistened in the sunlight, a healthy sheen over muscles that rippled with every movement. He had a reddish hue to his golden fur, darkest along his spine, almost like a ridgeback.

Aster moved back, giving her mate space to fight. He was fresh to battle and stood a better chance against Damian. If he was his alpha, there was a good chance they'd sparred together, or at least Gage had seen him fight before so he'd know Damian's weaknesses, if he had any. On the other hand, Damian would know Gage's shortcomings, too.

Suddenly, Gage leaped, and he succeeded where Aster had failed. Damian hissed when he was knocked sideways, but he rolled and quickly regained his footing. They circled each other, teeth on full display and each emitting a low, guttural growl. Gage pounced and forced Damian onto his back, but his jaws snapped open air as Damian managed to push Gage off. Suddenly, with a burst of speed, Damian attacked, and his teeth gained purchase on the back of Gage's neck.

Aster paced nervously along the perimeter of the open space, her tail swishing and twitching when she saw Gage begin to bleed. He broke free of Damian's hold and swatted at him with a paw the size of a baseball glove. Claws sliced through Damian's fur and skin like it was made of tissue paper. Fresh blood bubbled to the surface, and as the scent hit the air, several of the other shifter spectators grew restless. Damian began to slow down, succumbing to his multiple injuries, much to Aster's relief.

Minutes later, the fight was over. Gage began to dominate, and Damian's reaction time ebbed. Taking advantage of the hesitation, Gage tackled Damian and clamped his jaws shut. He made it look effortless when he ripped his alpha's throat out. Blood sprayed in an arc and pooled beneath the prone cat. After a shudder and a series of low pops, Damian's naked, human body lay on the grass. He was dead.

The relief of tension caused Aster's cat to retreat, now that the threat had been eliminated, and she shifted back to her human form. Her clothes had been reduced to shredded bits of fabric. She should have cared about being naked or the fact that practically half of the town had gathered to watch the fight, but she didn't, because Gage stood naked before her. The mating call wrapped around them like an invisible rope. They needed to go somewhere and fast; otherwise she was going to jump him right there.

She ran back to her apartment with Gage right beside her. She caught a glimpse of Willow standing outside Coffee Haven, a big, shit-eating grin on her face. Her tinkling laugh followed them when they turned into the deserted back alley. That's as far as they made it.

Aster had her foot on the bottom step when Gage's arms circled her waist, and he pulled her against him. His erection pressed against her.

"I need you now," he growled in her ear before nipping it with his teeth, sending another wave of arousal over her body. She shivered in anticipation, enjoying the feel of his skin against hers.

He stepped away and she turned around in his arms. Face to face with her mate, she licked her lips, and his blue eyes flared with need before he lowered his head and captured her mouth with his. His tongue slipped against hers, and she opened a little wider to accommodate him, deepening the kiss. His taste exploded on her tongue. The trace of Damian's blood that lingered excited her, called to her animal nature, and she pressed her body closer, her breasts crushed against his chest. Her mate had killed for her. He defended her and her family. Nothing was hotter than that.

"Thank you," she whispered before kissing him again. She looped her arms around his neck and stood on her tiptoes, half-tempted to climb up his body. Gage saved her the work when his calloused hands moved down to cup her ass, and in one fluid movement, he lifted her. Aster wrapped her long legs around his hips as he lowered her onto him. He filled her completely, and she moaned in pleasure as their connection deepened. They didn't move, just stayed still and enjoyed the moment of their union. Her heart beat in sync with her mate's, and the rhythm pounded deep, like it was in her bones. She licked his lips, little teasing laps with her tongue until they parted, and she was back to tasting him. His scent filled her nose and she tightened around him. The stillness was broken, and Gage started to move.

Aster held on tight and rode him as he rode her. Her nails dug into his shoulder, drawing blood. Dropping her head, she licked up the droplets, cleaning the tiny wounds. Once his blood hit her throat, she was lost and exploded around him. Gage cried out, and his thrusts slowed as he shuddered, releasing deep inside her. She rested her forehead in the crook of his neck, shaking, boneless, weak, and not trusting her legs to support her if he set her down. Gage didn't, though, and he carried her upstairs to her apartment.

CHAPTER 6

*A*ster woke a couple hours later, tangled in sheets and burning hot from Gage's body wrapped around her. She lay on her side and he behind her, but his right leg was between hers, effectively holding her in place. She moved slightly and rubbed against the top of his thigh, triggering instant arousal. She was sore and sticky from their lovemaking, but she couldn't get enough. It was never like this with Patrick or with anyone. Her cat and human sides were harmonious with the finding of her mate.

Gage mumbled in his sleep, and his arm that was draped across her side moved until his hand cupped her breast, then he quieted. His touch on her sensitive nipple was too much. Taking advantage of him being docile and sleepy, she rolled him onto his back and took him into her mouth. He was already semi-hard, and it didn't take long for him to wake up and tangle his fingers in her hair, holding her steady as he thrust deep. When she sensed he was close, she sat up and quickly straddled him, easing him past her tender entrance.

Afterward, she lay in his arms, sated and happy, and his fingers traced a lazy trail up and down her side. She felt guilty, though, at her happiness. It didn't change the fact that her brother was dead, her father wounded, and Patrick, too. She thought about how she would react if Gage had been hurt, and the very idea made her stomach flip and her heart ache. Is that how Reeve felt? Now that she understood the powerful and uncontrollable call of the true mate, she didn't harbor any ill will toward her sister. She needed to find her. She needed to go to her family. She needed to know more about Gage. There was so much to do. Life was too short, too precious to waste on anger, jealousy, and selfishness.

"Where are your thoughts going?" Gage asked.

Aster sat up and looked down at her mate. She had noticed the tattoo over his left pectoral, but had been too busy to ask him the meaning. It consisted of an intricate design in the background with a box featuring two crossed swords. At North, West and East points in between the sword blades, there were gold fleur de lis, and the southern point was an anchor. On top of this box was a medieval-style knight helmet. At the very top and bottom of the tattoo, there were two scrolls. The one at the bottom had Gage's surname, Barrows, and the top scroll contained two Latin words: Parum sufficit. Directly below this scroll was a stag's head. Aster traced the ink with a fingertip.

"What's the significance?" she asked.

"It's my family's coat of arms. Everyone in my family, when they turn eighteen, gets one."

"What does 'Parum sufficit' mean?"

"Little enough or a little is enough. It reminds us to stay humble and not live beyond our means or give into excess. My family dates back to the Old World. My ancestors came over from England in the 1700s."

"My ancestors came over from Ireland when the famine hit. Speaking of which, I need to go to my family. Will you come with me?"

"Of course, I'll be by your side from here on out." Gage sat up and pulled Aster onto his lap. She settled in with the familiarity of a couple who has been together for years, not strangers who just met. "I am yours," he said and kissed the tip of her nose.

"And I'm yours," she responded and with a reluctant sigh, climbed off of her mate. She needed to face her family and own up to her mistake that resulted in Braden's death. She didn't know how much damage she had caused and if it was irreparable.

They showered, and Aster dug up clothes that Patrick had left at her apartment. Gage had tracked Damian's scent to follow him, which required him to stay in cat form.

"Fortunately, I stumbled upon a plastic bag full of clothing stashed in a rotting tree trunk alongside the river. Otherwise, I'd have been strutting through town butt ass naked," he said when Aster handed him Patrick's clothes. The jeans were short in the leg and the polo shirt ridiculously tight, but she appreciated the view.

"If there's a store in town that sells clothes, I'd buy some, but I don't have my wallet," Gage said as they left her apartment.

"Don't worry about it. We'll stop at Backwoods Sport & Ski. They sell shoes, too." She looked down at his bare feet, and he wiggled his toes, making her laugh. They strolled hand in hand through the employee and delivery entrance of the coffee shop. Willow sat at one of the tables counting out the register, since Coffee Haven had closed for the day. She set the money in her hand down on the table and looked over at them.

"Well, hello, tall and handsome stranger. It's funny how I was just telling Aster to look forward to one of these in the near future . . . great timing," she said with a wink while patting her baby bump.

"Really?" Aster said, feeling the blush travel up her neck and bloom on her cheeks. "Gage, this is my boss, Willow."

She spied her bag behind the counter on a shelf beside the extra napkins and coffee stirrers. She also noticed a paper bag next to it with a little heart drawn on one side. She opened it to find two of her blueberry scones. She smiled and handed the bag to Gage.

"We have to go see my family, Willow. I'll catch up with you later." Aster leaned over and kissed Willow on the cheek.

"I understand, honey." Willow's earlier mischievousness disappeared, replaced with genuine concern. "Don't worry about work this week. I arranged it with Paisley so she can cover. You need time off for bereavement. I'm so sorry about Braden." Willow hoisted herself out of the chair, accepting Gage's assistance. "Take all the time you need." She pulled Aster into a hug and held her tight.

Aster felt the tears threaten to surface, and she blinked them away.

"Thanks," she said, her voice rough with emotion.

"By the way, Sheriff Kasun came by to talk to you. When I told him you just met your mate, he backed off."

"Thanks."

They left out the front door of the shop, which Aster locked behind them. They didn't have far to walk, since Backwoods Sport & Ski was also located on town square. When they passed by Shelf Indulgence, the bookstore right next to Coffee Haven, Aster glanced in one of the large windows and saw the owner, Sedona Matthews, sitting on her stool at the counter with her nose in a book. For a Monday, the town was busy. People were ducking in and out of shops. The beautiful, warm June day encouraged people to be outdoors. The trees lining the street and those in the town square were in full bloom, an incongruous sight with the snowcapped mountain range looming in the distance. A banner stretched across Main Street advertising the annual Midsummers Night festival that was taking place the following weekend. She looked forward to taking Gage and introducing him to one of Havenwood Falls' traditions for the supernatural community, where most of the humans were put to sleep and supes ran free.

Aster wandered through the women's section while Gage tried on some clothes. He emerged from the fitting room wearing a green T-shirt and dark blue jeans. Hiking boots completed the outfit. Aster used her credit card, and Gage promised to pay her back.

"I'm not worried. We take care of each other. That's how this works, right?" she said with a smile as he took the shopping bag from the cashier, who subtly sniffed his hand. Gage was new to town and sure to garner interest among the other shifters.

"I guess so," he agreed.

They walked around the corner to where her Nissan Sentra was parked. It was a college graduation present from her parents, and it still had the new-car smell. Aster kept it meticulously clean, too. She didn't pull out of the parking lot right away. She sat with the car idling and her hands on the steering wheel. The next stop was her parents' house and facing full acceptance of Braden's death.

"Hey," Gage placed a hand over hers. "I'll be there. I'm not going anywhere."

Aster started to cry. "You don't understand! Braden is dead because of me!" She dropped her head and sobbed, unable to look at Gage. He had no idea what a selfish creature he had just become mated to. "I sent Damian directly to Reeve out of spite because she took Patrick away, right in front of me. But it doesn't matter now, does it?"

"Hush, shh shh shh," Gage whispered, brushing her hair out of her face. It was still damp from the shower. "If it's anyone's fault, it's mine. I had no idea what Damian was up to. Did you know he had a collection of women he kept locked up in a house? Your sister was one of them."

"What?" This startling revelation stopped Aster's tears in their tracks. Her green eyes widened, and she finally looked at Gage.

"Yeah." Gage ran a hand through his short hair, and his jaw clenched. "Marta, who apparently worked at the house where they kept these prisoners, told me. She called me after your sister escaped, and Damian freaked out. He'd been collecting daughters of alphas, so his offspring would be superior or pureblooded, or some crazy shit like that."

"Oh my God! At the coffee shop, he made a comment about coming back to get me for his collection." She shuddered at the idea of being forced to mate with that monster, then her thoughts turned to Reeve. *What if Damian had raped her?* Concern for her sister overrode everything else, so she popped the Sentra in reverse and backed out of the parking spot.

On the way to her parents' house, they slowed down as they drove past Havenwood Village and saw several witches working with deputies interviewing witnesses. Aster knew they had isolated the visitors and humans from the crowd and were casting amnesia spells to erase their recollection of all they had witnessed. Devices would be wiped of videos and photos, too. She didn't see Sheriff Kasun, so she continued driving. When Gage bit into a scone, he groaned like he had an orgasm, a sound she was quickly becoming familiar with.

"Do you like?"

"Yes! This is hands down the best fucking scone I've ever had."

"I made them."

Gage looked at her with awe. "You made these? Damn, I love you. My mate has skills." He took another bite, practically shoving the entire scone in his mouth, and Aster laughed at his enthusiasm.

Aster's parents lived in Creekwood, a development that was about a five-minute drive from downtown Havenwood Falls. McCabe & Sons Construction, the company Aster's grandfather started, built Creekwood, from the country club to the home Aster grew up in. The upscale development was nestled among trees and separated from town by Mathews River. It was a pretty drive along a winding road that ran alongside the golf course.

The closer they got to her parents' house, the more anxious Aster became. Gage must have sensed it, because he reached across the console and placed his hand on her thigh. He gave it a light squeeze. His touch and the warmth from his hand did provide some comfort, and she relaxed her death grip on the steering wheel.

Cars lined the street outside her parents' house, and Aster recognized all of them. Her grandparents' Subaru Forester and her Uncle Paul's antique Ford pickup truck were in the driveway, and her sister-in-law's minivan was parked out front. Patrick's Jeep and Sheriff Kasun's unmarked black truck were across the street. Aster pulled to a stop behind the minivan and put her car in park, but didn't get out right away.

"Hell of a way to meet my family," she said to Gage and was just about ready to tell him that Braden would probably pull his protective big brother nonsense and to ignore him. Even though she stopped herself from saying anything, the thoughts were there, a reminder that Braden was gone. Sighing deeply, Aster turned to her mate. "Ready?"

They walked up the winding driveway, lined with tiny solar lights that were still charging, as the sun had yet to dip behind the mountain range to the west. Her parents' house was a large two-story made primarily of gray stone with wood trim and features. Large windows faced the street, and Aster could see her family moving around inside. Lupines and hydrangea were in full bloom and lined the walkway that led to the front door.

She stepped inside the house to a low murmur of several conversations going on at once. The noise didn't cover up the sound of someone sobbing. Aster looked around for the source and saw her sister-in-law, Kaitlyn, sitting on the loveseat. Aster's grandmother was consoling her, while Braden and Kaitlyn's son was curled up in a ball and asleep on the other end. His thumb was in his mouth, his eyelids puffy from crying. At three years old, he was old enough to know something bad had happened, but too young to really understand. He was also the spitting image of his father, with reddish brown hair and a scattering of freckles across his nose. Her heart broke all over again seeing them, and she buried her face in Gage's chest to muffle her sobs.

He guided her farther into the house. The living room was to the right of the wide entryway where Aster and Gage stood. A large ceiling fan circled overhead, suspended from the high ceiling. To the left was the dining room that held a dark wood dining room table. At one end, Sheriff Kasun sat with Reeve, Patrick, and her father. They were deep in conversation, and the sheriff took notes in a leather-bound notebook. Aster moved to join them, but was stopped by her mom, who was descending the stairs. Her face was pale and drawn, her green eyes ringed with red. Seeing the grief etched on her mom caused Aster to cry out and run to her. Anne met her at the bottom of the stairs and pulled her into an embrace. They held each other and sobbed.

"I'm so sorry, Mom!" Aster choked out when they separated. "It's all my fault."

"Shhhh, what are you talking about? Come, let's talk." Anne guided Aster into the kitchen, and she gestured for Gage to follow. A fresh pot of coffee brewed, filling the air with its rich aroma. They sat down in a dining nook surrounded by windows, and it seemed as though the area was filled with sunlight and glowed like they were in a sun globe.

Gage sat down next to Aster and took her left hand while Anne sat down on the other side.

"And who are you?" Anne asked him.

"Gage Bellows, ma'am. I'm, uh, well, I'm Aster's mate."

Surprise and shock registered on her face before she smiled at him.

"What good news to receive on such a sad day." She reached across the table and placed her hand on top of their joined ones. "How remarkable that both of my daughters find their mates within days of each other—I'm so happy for you both. Now," she sat up and withdrew her hand, focusing her attention back on Aster. "Your father and Sheriff Kasun need to talk to you and Gage. The sheriff needs to give full reports to the Court and Mayor Stuart. What happened today violated so many laws and risked exposing the town's secrets. Then you two, streaking down Main Street like horny teenagers on spring break, didn't help either. The cleanup and damage control are massive. Braden's death and that other shifter, well, that's the worst of all that happened. Your sister and Patrick are giving their statements now. Apparently, this shifter knew Reeve from Denver and followed her here?"

"Yes, ma'am. Damian was my alpha. I followed him here to stop him from doing anything crazy. Unfortunately, I got here too late. I'm so sorry about your son."

Anne's eyes shone with tears that she blinked away. Seemingly at a loss for words, she patted his hand and gave it a squeeze before glancing toward the entrance to the kitchen.

Mike McCabe limped into the room, and Aster looked up at him, preparing for him to chew her ass out. Instead he held his arms open. His face, already showing wear from years spent out in the sun on job sites, had aged in just the past few hours. Grief had already left its mark. Aster flew into his arms, and he wrapped her up tight in a bear hug that immediately transported her back to when she was a little girl who sought out her dad's comfort. She always felt tiny in comparison to his hulking size. At over six-foot-two, with a barrel chest and shoulders broad enough to carry the weight of the world, "Big Mike" McCabe lived up to his nickname.

"Baby girl, I'm so glad you're okay. When I saw you charge in to fight, I thought you were going to be killed, too," her dad said into her hair, before stepping away and holding her at arm's length so he could inspect her for any damage.

With the exception of a bruise on her shoulder from when she hit the ground, she was fine. Her father, however, looked like he had been in a fight with a tree shredder. His weather-beaten face was covered with scratches and nicks. A large gash over his right eyebrow had been stitched up. The black stitches resembled an insect perched above his eye. Thick brown hair, graying at the temples, curled around his ears, revealing the one missing lobe, a wound from years ago. He was a study of old and new battles. While they were shifters and possessed supernatural strength, they still healed at the rate of humans and retained scars from their injuries.

"Dad, I'm so sorry about everything!" Aster cried out. Seeing his injuries brought everything surging forth. She could have lost him, too.

"Hush, baby girl, it's not your fault. Damian Stone killed your brother, not you. This isn't your burden to bear." He held her as she cried. Her face pressed against his polo shirt, which absorbed her tears. A hand came to rest on the small of her back, the warmth instantly seeping through her shirt, and she was already familiar with this touch. Her mate. Gage wanted to provide comfort too.

She stepped out of her dad's embrace, and Gage moved forward to introduce himself, explaining his connection to Damian. "I wish we were meeting under better circumstances," he said.

"You saved Aster. Thank you. You're one hell of a fighter. It couldn't have been easy, going up against your alpha."

Gage nodded in agreement. "I own a gym called the Sweat Box, where I train MMA fighters, plus I've been Damian's beta for the past three-and-a-half years. We fought side by side countless times, but I never had to fight against him. For a split second, I hesitated, but when I saw Aster in danger, any hesitation evaporated. She's all I care about now."

Big Mike grinned at this comment. "Mates—it's a powerful bond. One look at Aster's mom, and I was done for."

Just then, Reeve and Patrick filed into the kitchen, followed by Sheriff Kasun, who was hard to miss. While not much taller than her father, Sheriff Kasun was as wide as a refrigerator and solid muscle. Reeve's right arm was wrapped in gauze, and blood had already oozed through—pinkish red stripes, an imprint of the claw marks concealed beneath. Her bottom lip was split and already beginning to scab over, and the beginnings of a black eye shadowed the left side of her face. Patrick hobbled in on crutches, his leg in an air cast, and his face didn't fare much better than her father's.

Aster wanted to run to her sister and pull her into a hug, beg for forgiveness, but she wasn't sure if that would be welcome. Reeve made the first move and pulled Aster into a fierce hug.

"Forgive me?" Reeve asked, stealing Aster's line.

"What for? I'm the one who's been such a spiteful, petty asshole." This admission made Reeve laugh, and the hug tightened.

"I did take your man," Reeve said, and Aster shrugged. Now that she'd found her mate, the hurt and anger she had experienced earlier were long gone.

They separated, but stood side by side with their arms wrapped around each other's waists, and their heads were tilted, resting against each other. With less than a half-inch difference in height and similar builds, and with their hair the same color, they could have passed as twins.

"Can we go talk?" Reeve asked. "I have something to tell you, something I should have told you a long time ago."

"Of course." As they left everyone behind in the kitchen and climbed the stairs, Aster tried to puzzle out what her sister had to say.

Her bedroom hadn't changed much, and it was like stepping back in time. Her old twin bed still had the sea-foam green comforter and matching bed skirt. Framed pictures of her senior year were mounted on the wall, and miniature pompoms, in Havenwood Falls High's silver and blue, hung on the bedpost, a memento from a homecoming game. One side of the room had a poster for AFI, her favorite band,

and a family portrait taken when she was twelve, Reeve was fourteen, and Braden eighteen.

Seeing her brother's smiling face and mischievous eyes made her heart ache. She sank down on the side of her bed, and Reeve sat next to her. She, too, was looking at the picture. They were all happy and whole then. Reeve had just started high school, and Aster was in middle school. This was taken before they fought all the time and before Aster's jealousy turned into resentment. It didn't even matter now, and looking back, all of it was so stupid. She had lost so much valuable time.

"Aster, I want us to get along. I really want to try. Now that Braden is gone," Reeve's voice cracked, and Aster looked over to see her sister crying. "It's just us, you know?"

"I know. I want to try, too, and I'm done being jealous of you. I was an asshole."

"You already said that." Her laugh was shaky, but it was a laugh and a positive start. "I left Havenwood Falls for you. That's what I wanted to tell you."

Aster's eyebrows rose, and she stared at her sister in amazement. "What are you talking about?"

"I knew you were miserable, and we fought constantly. I originally had planned to stay home and take online classes after graduating high school, but thought going away for college would give us the space we needed. So, Dad asked for approval from the Court for me to leave to attend UC Denver, but he petitioned to have the memory spell lifted so I could still come home and not forget anyone. I swore an oath to never reveal Havenwood Falls or bring anyone back without the Court's permission."

"Reeve . . ." Aster started, but didn't know what to say. Her sister's leaving was an act of selflessness, which made her feel all the more selfish. *It doesn't matter anymore,* she reminded herself. She leaned over and rested her head on her sister's shoulder. "Despite how I acted, I always loved you," she admitted.

"I love you, too."

They sat together like that in silence, enjoying the moment.

"Braden would have loved to see this," Aster said a couple of minutes later. "He was always stuck in the middle, trying to broker some sort of peace agreement between us."

"Right? Like we're the Middle East or something . . . brave soul for getting between two redheads, though," Reeve said with a chuckle that faded into a sigh. "I can't believe he's gone."

"Me, either." This time they leaned against each other for support as they wept and mourned over the loss of their brother.

This is where their mates found them. Aster looked up when they walked into the bedroom. This was her first time really seeing them next to each other, and she marveled at how similar they were in build and coloring. They could have passed for brothers, with their sandy light brown hair and height. Gage's upper body was more muscular and defined, but Patrick wasn't that much smaller. Gage sat down next to Aster, and Patrick sat down next to Reeve.

"I gave my statement to the sheriff," Gage told Aster. "Are you ready to talk to him?"

She nodded and stood up, grabbing Gage's hand in the process so he'd go with her. She turned back to address her sister. "Thank you. See you downstairs?"

"Anything for you, sissy," Reeve responded with a wink and teasing smile when she used the nickname from when Aster was really little. "We'll be down in a bit."

Patrick had a hand on Reeve's thigh that kept creeping higher. The higher it went, the redder her cheeks became.

Aster rolled her eyes and tugged on Gage's hand.

"We're so out of here!" she yelled over her shoulder before shutting the door behind them.

Sheriff Kasun was waiting for Aster in the dining room. She took a seat across from him. The table had been recently polished, and the faint lemon scent clung to the wood. She clasped her hands in front of her, and they cast a blurry reflection on the finish. The sheriff regarded her with his piercing blue eyes that she had long been convinced could see right into people's souls.

"Aster, first I want to tell you I'm sorry about your brother. He was a good man."

Aster looked away, blinking fast to keep the tears at bay. Her throat ached from crying so much, and her head felt like it was full of cotton, her sinuses were so jacked.

"He . . . he was." Aster winced when she said this, hating to refer to Braden in the past tense.

"Can you tell me when you first encountered Damian Stone?" he asked, his pen poised over his notepad.

CHAPTER 7

Court of the Sun and the Moon, One Week Later

The Court of the Sun and the Moon held their hearings in the basement of City Hall in a windowless, soundproof room. In homage to the founders, the only lights used were candles. Large glass globes hung suspended from the wood-paneled ceiling, and each held white candles. Flickering flames cast shadows that danced on the walls, which were decorated with murals depicting a timeline of Havenwood Falls' history.

Aster sat at a table facing the Court, who sat on a raised dais, set up similar to a regular courtroom. Having all of the members of the Court, representatives of the town's Old Families, elevated before her was an imposing sight, and Aster licked her lips nervously. She tried not to stare too long at Willow's great-grandfather, Elmsed, who was the fae representative on the Court. He had lowered his glamour, so the arrow-shaped tips of his ears were clearly visible, poking through his silver hair. His nose was almost flat, and his long chin almost touched his chest. He had frosty blue preternatural eyes, even more piercing than Sheriff Kasun's, and Aster felt pinned to her seat when his gaze fell upon her.

Aster was flanked by her dad and Gage, and Reeve and Patrick sat on the other side of Big Mike. They'd endured their inquisitions earlier, and the Court, anxious to not draw the proceedings out and potentially delay the Midsummers Night festivities, called them all into the room together for the verdict.

They all faced punishment for violating the rule prohibiting shifting in public. They had also been charged with engaging in a public fight in their shifter forms. Their actions had resulted in enlisting extra witches and mages to wipe devices and memories of any evidence.

Since Gage didn't register when he first arrived in town, he was originally going to have to face punishment for that offense, but he didn't know the rule, and he registered as soon as he became aware, so they threw the charge out.

"Aster Marjorie McCabe, please stand and come forward," Elmsed ordered. Gage's hand had been on her leg, and he gave her thigh an encouraging squeeze before she stood. On unsteady legs, she walked the few steps to stand in front of the court.

Mayor Barbie Stuart leaned over the dais; her body cast a shadow over Aster. The mayor was allegedly pure human, but the town's comedians speculated that she had giant genes in her DNA. She was almost the same size as Sheriff Kasun, and everything about her was big, from her hair to her chest.

"Aster, what do you and Gage plan to do now? Are you going to stay in Havenwood Falls?" she asked.

This question surprised her. They'd been so caught up with Braden's funeral and then the inquisitions that they'd never really talked about it. Gage was expected to return to Denver to restore order to his den. Since he was the one who killed Damian, he had inherited the leadership. The very thought of Gage leaving her behind while he took care of this business was as unpalatable as eating cockroaches. She turned around and looked at Gage. He, too, appeared surprised at the question.

"What happens if I choose to leave and go back to Denver with Gage?" she asked, facing the Court again.

"We discussed this. Eloise Sinclair predicted you would choose to go with your mate. However, this won't excuse you from any punishment." Eloise was a powerful psychic who owned Into the Mystic New Age Books and Gifts. She did psychic readings at the back of her store and ran a psychic fair every year. She had a steady clientele, because her predictions were accurate.

"If you leave Havenwood Falls, you can't come back for two years, and we won't remove the amnesia spell like we did for your sister. Your friends and family can't contact you either, not that you'd remember who they were if they did make an attempt."

Aster gasped and spun around to look at her father. His expression didn't convey any emotion, but his hands were clasped in front of him on the table, and she noticed his knuckles turning white. Leaving now that her family was still reeling from Braden's death was wrong, but staying behind and being separated from her mate wasn't right, either.

"You know the rules, Aster, and you broke them. We can't be lenient with anyone. Order needs to be a constant, otherwise we devolve into chaos."

"What's the punishment if I stay?" she asked.

"Gage engaged in a public fight in his cat form before even registering here, which sets a poor precedent for his den. He'll be banished permanently, and you, Aster, will serve a three-month sentence in jail."

Elsmed stared down at Aster with his frosty eyes. Sweat gathered under her hair as he stared at her. Beads slid down her neck and underneath her blouse, to collect at the small of her back. Neither option was ideal, but punishments weren't meant to be easy. She did fuck up. On the surface, the second option seemed to be the better one. Being separated from Gage would suck and possibly be physically painful, like withdrawing from a drug, but how bad could three months be? His permanent banishment was an issue. She'd want to be able to come back for holidays and family occasions, especially once they started having children. She wanted Gage to be included. Two years away from her home and the only place she'd ever lived was a long time. Sure she went on vacations, but always returned within the first twenty-eight days, before the amnesia spell took effect. What if after her two years was up she never felt the call to return to Havenwood Falls? Her family and her memories would be lost to her; all she'd have would be a new life with her mate. This was a risk with either option, though. Once she left Havenwood Falls and the amnesia spell kicked in, there weren't any guarantees she'd ever make it back . . . unless someone compelled her to return.

"You have twenty-four hours to choose the punishment, Ms. McCabe. I think we've been more than generous, considering."

She had a lot to think about, but didn't have the time right then, as the Court had moved on to reading off the other punishments. Elsmed called Gage to the front of the dais, and Aster gave his hand a reassuring squeeze when he stood up.

"Mr. Barrows, you're new to Havenwood Falls and therefore not familiar with our rules. The circumstances of your arrival are extenuating, however, secrets have been revealed, and a life taken in public. Granted, a wild animal attack story is plausible and easy to sell, but the supernatural community knows better. From what we've learned about Damian Stone, many have argued that you performed a service. Stone killed one of our own, and his punishment would have been death."

Aster's heart jumped at that statement. *Did the Court plan on sentencing Gage to death—a life for a life?* She squirmed in her seat, ready to leap up and protest if that turned out to be the case. Elsmed peered down his flat nose and bided his time, like he enjoyed drawing out the suspense.

Aster barely breathed as she waited.

"You won't have the same fate," Elsmed finally said, and Aster exhaled in relief. "Gage Bellows, the Court sentences you to pay a penalty of fifty thousand dollars, and you will be held in jail until the fine is paid. Additionally, the memory spell will ensure you have no recollection of your visit here. We expect you not to linger once your fine is paid."

"Understood, and thank you for your fairness. I can make

payment arrangements immediately." Gage bowed to the Court before returning to his seat.

"You have fifty grand lying around to pay that fine?" Aster asked. Her eyebrows rose in surprise.

"I've done all right for myself," he answered, giving her a coy smile that revealed the adorable dimple in his left cheek she had grown to love. "Let's just say that the fight nights at my gym do really well."

The past couple of days had been days of discovery, and there was still a lot she didn't know about her mate. Since he didn't get sentenced to death, they had their whole lives to learn about each other.

Next, Reeve was called to the front. Aster pulled her attention away from Gage and his dimple. Her sister had dressed demurely for the occasion in a simple gray suit with a white shirt underneath. From where Aster sat, she could see Reeve shaking with nervousness, and Aster knew why. Reeve took full responsibility for bringing Damian Stone to Havenwood Falls. After sharing a bottle of wine and several crying jags following Braden's funeral, Reeve had revealed to Aster that she blamed herself for their brother's death. If she hadn't been followed, Braden would still be alive.

"Reeve McCabe, you know your crimes. Are you ready to accept your punishment without complaint?" Mayor Stuart asked.

"Yes. I will honor your decision," Reeve said, her voice so soft that Aster could barely hear it.

"Good. We will proceed. You are being charged with shifting and fighting in public as well as bringing a stranger—a dangerous stranger at that—to Havenwood Falls without seeking prior approval from the Court. You took an oath of secrecy before you left, and you broke that oath. For these crimes, you and your mate, Patrick O'Shea, will be sentenced to banishment."

"No!" Aster yelled, jumping up out of her seat and launching herself across the table. She shook off both her dad and Gage when they attempted to pull her back. She came to a stop next to her sister and reached for her hand. "Reeve never told that psycho about Havenwood Falls, and she was running for her life. How was she supposed to know that he would track her here? Plus, Patrick was acting in self-defense. You can't banish them!"

"While I admire you being loyal to your sister, she agreed to accept. Our decision is final."

"No," Aster whispered, more to herself than in protest, and she turned to Reeve who remained stoic in front of the Court with her head held high, but the glimmer of tears in her green eyes told another story.

Barbie rapped the gavel and told them to take a seat, then their father was called up. He faced the Court with his back straight, hands joined behind his back and his legs hip-width apart.

"Michael," Barbie began. "When you approached us six years ago to call in the favor we owed you, you do recall we were hesitant to honor your request because of something like this happening, correct?"

"Yes, Mayor, I know you all took a risk, and it was greatly appreciated."

Aster didn't like seeing her dad so acquiescent. He usually commanded the room and demanded respect.

"Clearly we all failed when we allowed the memory spell lifted from Reeve, but you called in your favor, so we had to honor it."

Gage leaned over and whispered in Aster's ear, "What did your dad do to earn a favor?"

"I have no idea, but I'm determined to find out," she replied and hoped the adage "curiosity killed the cat" didn't hold true.

"The Court has decided that having both of your daughters banished, on top of losing Braden, is punishment enough. Court adjourned." With a crack of the gavel, all members of the Court stood and silently filed out of the room through a side door that appeared in the middle of a mural depicting a dragon shifter melting down gold from the mines. The door disappeared once all of the members had passed through.

No one else moved. Mike McCabe had sunk back down in his chair and now stared off into the distance, his expression once again unreadable.

"Dad? What was this favor you had called in? It must have been pretty big."

"Not now, Aster," he said and pinched the bridge of his nose.

"Come on, Dad. I think we deserve to know, since all of our lives have been impacted. Besides, we're all adults now," Reeve pried.

"Fine!" he snapped and threw his hands up in the air. "I can't give specifics, but I will say that the Court has a lot of secrets and a lot of power. In order to protect our town, and our own kind, sometimes we have to make sacrifices and do things we don't want to do, but must. Anyway, because of things I've done for the Court, they bestowed one favor for me to use."

"They sound like the mafia," Aster said.

"Be careful what you say, baby girl. You're in enough trouble already, and you never know who is listening."

"Why did you risk telling us anything?" Reeve asked.

"Because you're all going to be leaving and will forget this information as well as everything else." At this admission, her dad's emotionless façade broke. He pulled Aster and Reeve into a hug, and they all sobbed. When they regained their composure, Aster wiped her eyes and had a thought.

"Dad, why do you assume I'll be leaving? I haven't given the court my decision yet."

He smiled at her and reached out to brush an errant tear from her cheek. "Baby girl, I know because you won't be able to leave your mate. As much as I know you want to be loyal to your family, you'll be miserable. Gage is your fate and your love. As Patrick is yours, Reeve," he said as he patted Reeve's knee. "I am going to miss you both so much, but I know you will be happy."

Aster turned to look at Gage, who stood off to the side watching her. Wordlessly he walked over and took her hand in his.

The next day, Aster delivered her decision to the Court.

GAGE DROVE Aster's Sentra through downtown Denver, pointing out landmarks along the way. Night had fallen by the time they hit the city limits, and the skyline was lit up like Christmas. Aster marveled at the height of the skyscrapers that had been built around older buildings like Union Station, its bright orange sign visible for miles.

"Oh, there's my work!" Reeve announced from the backseat. Aster looked in the direction her sister pointed and saw a sleek three-story building. A giant monitor in the front glass window displayed images of fancy events. "I'll talk to the owner about hiring you, Aster. Your scones will be a huge hit."

While the Court had banished them from Havenwood Falls, they didn't put any restrictions on where they had to go. Maybe the loophole was intentional or an oversight, but Aster and Reeve saw it as a gift. At least they could be banished together. After a tearful farewell, Aster, Gage, Reeve, and Patrick were on their way. When they left Havenwood Falls, Aster had looked in the side view mirror at her parents. They had stood in the middle of the street waving goodbye, and Aster watched until they faded from view, then she focused her attention on the journey ahead.

Gage had Damian's mess to clean up, and he needed to assert himself as the new alpha quickly. How deep the faction of species purists ran in the den remained to be seen. When Reeve described her time as a captive and mentioned that other women were being held prisoner, too, it chilled Aster to the bone. Historically, species purists went to great lengths to achieve their goals, and Damian wasn't an exception.

As if she was thinking the same thing, Reeve asked Gage why Damian had never told him about his breed purity project.

"I don't know," Gage answered. Aster noticed he made eye contact with Reeve using the rearview mirror. "But, I think he knew I'd object to his plans and challenge him. He also knew that he stood a good chance of losing to me."

They dropped Reeve and Patrick off at Reeve's apartment. Her sister's landlord had made arrangements with the doorman to let her in since she'd lost her keys. With a promise to meet up for dinner the next day, Aster and Gage continued on to his house. She looked over at her mate as he concentrated on the road and navigated through traffic. She examined his profile—the straight nose and long lashes, how his lower lip stuck out a little bit in a permanent pout that she loved to nibble on. His big hands were loose and didn't grip the steering wheel tightly, indicating his confidence with driving. She had only known Gage for a little more than a week, but she already knew him to be a strong leader and fierce protector.

Whatever lay ahead, they would face it together.

WE HOPE you enjoyed this story in the Havenwood Falls series of novellas featuring a variety of supernatural creatures. The series is a collaborative effort by multiple authors. Each book is generally a stand-alone, so you can read them in any order, although some authors will be writing sequels to their own stories. Please be aware when you choose your next read.

Other books in the main Havenwood Falls series:

Forget You Not by Kristie Cook

Old Wounds by Susan Burdorf

Covetousness by Randi Cooley Wilson

Coming soon are books by Lila Felix, R.K. Ryals, Belinda Boring, Heather Hildenbrand, Stacey Rourke, and more.

WATCH FOR HAVENWOOD FALLS HIGH, a Young Adult series launching in October 2017.

IMMERSE yourself in the world of Havenwood Falls and stay up to date on news and announcements at www.HavenwoodFalls.com. Join our reader group, Havenwood Falls Book Club, on Facebook at https://www.facebook.com/groups/HavenwoodFallsBookClub/

ABOUT THE AUTHOR

E.J. Fechenda has lived in Philadelphia and Phoenix, and now calls Portland, Maine home. She is the Amazon bestselling author of The New Mafia Trilogy and is currently working on the Ghost Stories Trilogy. She has a degree in Journalism from Temple University and her short stories have been published in *Suspense Magazine* and several anthologies. E.J. is a member of the Maine Writers and Publishers Alliance and co-founder of the fiction reading series, "Lit: Readings & Libations", which is held semi-quarterly in Portland.

You can find her on the internet here:
Facebook: https://www.facebook.com/EJFechendaAuthor
Twitter @ebusjaneus (https://twitter.com/ebusjaneus)
Tumblr: http://ejfechenda.tumblr.com/

ACKNOWLEDGMENTS

I need to give a huge shout out to Kristie Cook for coming up with the incredible concept of Havenwood Falls and for keeping the crazy train on the tracks. Keeping all the stories and elements straight, plus herding multiple authors, is serious work, and she makes it seem so easy. This is a tremendous opportunity, and I'm excited to be included. It's been a blast collaborating with the other authors on this project such as Kallie Ross, Kristen Yard, Randi Cooley Wilson, Belinda Boring, and so many more. Some of their characters and businesses are mentioned in Fate, Loyalty & Love. I'd like to thank Liz Ferry for working her proofreading magic. My husband deserves huge props because I basically ignored him on his birthday to work on revisions. He always helps to keep me on task, and at one point said, "Go pursue your passion!" So, yeah, he earned this acknowledgment. To all of my family, friends, and fans, thank you for your support and enthusiasm. When my tank is running on empty, you help fill it back up. Much love!

~ A Havenwood Falls New Adult Novella ~

Havenwood Falls

Covetousness

RANDI COOLEY WILSON

Covetousness (A Havenwood Falls Novella) by Randi Cooley Wilson

Graysin Ravenal hasn't seen her sister in years, but when she learns Jenni has mysteriously died in a library fire, she leaves her upscale beach community for the mountains of Colorado in search of answers. She needs a job, and Havenwood Falls happens to need an interior designer for the new library. The last thing she needs, though, is to fall for the dark and sexy Everett Weston, aka her new boss.

Their undeniable mutual attraction aside, keeping their relationship professional proves impossible as their lives collide in more ways than one.

Graysin finds herself immersed in a world heavily guarded by secrets and lies—a world Everett seems to know quite well, making him her only hope in finding the answers she seeks. As they work together to unlock the mystery surrounding Jenni's death, their ever-increasing passion must be denied, no matter what their hearts say. Because the story they're thrown into is one of desire and danger that not only uncovers a centuries old secret that could destroy the town, but also reveals the darkness of Graysin's family's past—a darkness that changes her life forever. And some secrets just can't be forgiven.

COVETOUSNESS

AN EXCERPT

*M*y breath comes out in billowy white puffs as I exhale into the cold evening air. A light blanket of fog has crept though the darkness surrounding me. The forest creaks and groans with each gust of wind that passes through it. My gaze follows the sway of the trees, and I shiver as the counter on the outdated gas pump climbs. All around me, there is an unnatural energy that crackles in the air.

In some remote corner of my consciousness, a whisper creeps in, telling me that I should have stayed on the interstate. The wind lifts again, causing another shudder to run through me as the nozzle's clip snaps and echoes, stopping the flow of liquid and alerting me that my tank is full.

After returning the spout to the pump, I tighten the cap and make my way toward the run-down, dated station to pay. The glass door chimes as I push into the small space and look around.

The smell of tobacco assaults my nose, causing it to twitch. Overhead, a fluorescent light buzzes and hums, and its glow barely brings into focus the ancient-looking Native American gentleman seated behind the counter. He's watching me with a strange, guarded fascination.

I offer him a kind smile. He responds by blowing a puff of tobacco smoke from his wooden pipe into my face. *Lovely.* His chocolate gaze slides to the grimy window, and he stares at my shiny Range Rover.

"Guess you're not from around here." His voice is deep and raspy.

"What gives you that impression?" I ask, approaching him.

The older man just focuses on my car with displeasure. "It's not a Jeep."

I shift, feeling uncomfortable. "It was a graduation gift. From design school."

Unimpressed, he ignores my justification. "That will be $38.22."

With a sigh, I dig into my bag, searching for my wallet.

"You got all-wheel drive on your fancy ride, young lady?"

I frown at the term, handing him two twenties. "Yes."

"That's good. You'll need it up here in the mountains." He opens the manual cash register and counts out my change at a snail's pace. "Western Colorado is a long way from Rhode Island."

My brows pinch at his uncanny knowledge and inquisitive manner.

"Your license plate." He points at my car when he notices my confusion.

"It is," I reply.

His white, bushy eyebrows drop over his stare as he studies me with a piercing look. Ignoring his odd behavior, I take my change from his rough and wrinkled hand.

"Do I know you?" he asks, watching me. "You look . . . familiar."

At his words, a heavy sadness falls over me. "Not likely. I'm new around here."

A dip of his chin is his only answer before his focus slides to the door—my cue to leave.

"Have a nice evening," I mutter, because politeness has been ingrained into me.

The stranger doesn't respond immediately. He just looks me over with guarded curiosity.

"Drive safely. You wouldn't want to get lost out here." His voice follows me out the door.

Once I'm securely in my vehicle, I exhale my nervous energy, push the on button, and blast the heat. Before I pull out, my gaze shifts to the rearview mirror that reflects the station, but it's gone completely dark and the old man is nowhere in sight.

I try not to peel out of the unpaved lot as I make my way back onto the main road. My GPS stopped working about an hour ago, and I hope to hell I'm going in the right direction. I probably should have stopped two hours earlier in Grand Junction for the night, but I just wanted to get there already. Days on the road alone will do that to you —make you antsy to arrive in a place filled with strangers. One that you've never been to, and barely know anything about.

Frowning, I lean back into the soft leather of the bucket seat, already missing the ocean. The coastal community of Newport, Rhode Island, is nothing like the forested mountains of Colorado.

Everything here is pitch black, especially the road in front of me. I can't figure out the allure.

A soft melody comes on the radio—at least that still works—as I make my way up the long, narrow mountain road. The moon disappeared long ago, leaving the darkness in its place.

Trying to keep my mind off the eerie feeling I have, I think of home. The ghost of her presence lingers, haunting each of my memories and thoughts. I feel her everywhere. Even now, as I stare into the blackness of the night, driving toward a new fate. A new life.

After receiving my degree in interior architecture and arts from the Rhode Island School of Design, I was only able to secure a few local jobs. In the upscale community I grew up in, there is no shortage of interior designers. The couple of assignments I did manage to snag were with bored wives who needed a distraction while their husbands were off golfing or yachting.

A graduate with fresh, modern design ideas isn't necessarily welcome in a community full of old money and country club homes, covered with toile wallpaper and matching throw pillows.

At the thought, I blow out a long breath.

Finally, after multiple email exchanges with my new employer, here I am—driving at an ungodly hour, on a dark, winding, forest road toward a mountain town that I've only heard about in brief, nonsensical phone conversations—on my way to work for a small design firm. And to find answers.

I clutch the steering wheel as I drive by a layered stone sign, lit by a single spotlight. The black metal lettering lets me know I'm a few miles away from my destination.

"Thanks for all the help," I pout at my GPS.

Grabbing my cell, I glance at it and frown.

No service. *Fabulous.*

I'm in the middle of nowhere, in the dead of night, with no cell. Sighing, I throw it back onto the passenger seat, where it bounces and lands on the floor. Keeping my eyes on the road, I reach down to grab it, just as something large, dark, and furry jumps in front of my car, scaring the shit out of me. I jerk the wheel quickly to avoid hitting what appears to be an oversized wolf.

My car skids as I slam on the brakes, trying to gain control. The sound of rocks crunching and crumbling under my tires echoes around the forest. With a final slide, one of my tires releases a loud pop before I come to a complete stop, and I watch as the front right side of the car begins to sink, signaling my tire just blew out.

"Mother-effer," I shout, and hit the steering wheel with my palm.

After a few heavy breaths, I look up and see two brown eyes with gold flecks staring at me.

Directly. At. Me. *Holy shit.*

It almost appears as if the reddish-brown wolf is watching me, entertained.

I swear its eyes twinkle with amusement before it winks at me. *Wait. What the . . .*

Deep breaths. Get your shit together, Graysin. Do not panic. The wild animal is NOT winking at you.

The sudden, heavy pounding of a fist banging on my window causes me to jump and scream.

Scared to death, I pull my eyes away from the enormous animal before snapping my attention to the driver's side window. Deep, lush, verdant eyes are peering at me through the tinted glass.

"Hey, you okay in there?" the stranger asks.

Still shocked, my focus darts back to the wild animal, but it's gone. *What in the—*

"Hello? Miss?" The almost glowing eyes glisten.

Swallowing, I regain my composure and nod that I'm okay.

"While I appreciate that you're in shock, there is a thick layer of dark glass in between us. If you're bleeding or hurt, I'll need some verbal cues here," he states in a smooth yet annoyed voice.

I exhale, unsure what he's doing out here in the middle of the woods at this hour. Seconds ago, no one was even around. Peering in the rearview mirror, I notice the headlight of a motorcycle parked behind my car. Surely I would have heard its rumble behind me, right?

Disoriented, I sneak another peek at the stranger who is bent over, trying to see into the car. His large hands are cupped around his eyes —as if that is going to help him gain a better view.

Two leather bands peak out from his leather jacket, wrapped around his wrists, which I find extremely attractive. After a moment, he runs a hand through his dark, thick hair. It's short on the sides, curly on the top, and messily wind-blown. It's sexy. Light scruff accentuates what appears to be a perfect jawline.

I press the window button and let the glass drop down just a sliver. In case this unusually good-looking stranger is a serial killer and all. Seriously, he is otherworldly handsome.

I've never seen anything like it; he's practically shining.

"Are you an angel or something?" I blurt out in a mumble.

He frowns, watching me. "Did you hit your head?"

Realizing I'd spoken my thoughts out loud, I swallow and grimace at myself.

"Um . . . no," I manage, trying to hide the shake in my voice.

His radiant orbs study me. "Are you sure?"

I assess my body, but other than being scared to death, I'm good.

"Yup. See?" I motion to myself. "I am *fine*." I cringe. The words are more seductive than I meant them to be.

The stranger's gaze twinkles with an arrogant amusement before he looks at the front of my car. "You have a spare?"

"A spare car? No. This is the only one I own . . ." I trail off when I notice he's staring at me.

"I meant a spare *tire*. You drove over some rocks back there, and they pierced the rubber."

My eyelids slide closed. *God.* Could I be any more of a spaz? "Right. Under the car."

We sit in silence for a moment before he stands. "I'll need access to your trunk."

When he realizes I'm confused by his statement, he sighs.

"So I can get to the jack? I'll undress it—the *tire*, that is," he adds for clarification.

"I understood what you meant," I blurt out, too quickly.

He smirks cockily. "Sure you did," he counters, with a slight Spanish accent.

I roll my eyes, and he lets out another sigh as I study him, wondering if I should trust him.

He tightens his jaw. "Look, if it will make you feel more comfortable, you can sit in the car, and I'd be happy to replace the tire for you."

"Um . . . I can just call roadside assistance."

He stares at me. "Where are you headed anyway at this hour?"

"Havenwood Falls."

"Havenwood Falls?" The stranger repeats in an odd tone, studying me. "Well, there's crappy cell service out here, in and around the town. It's a quirk this high up in the mountains."

"Oh." I glance longingly at my cell, still on the floor, with no signal.

"Looks like I'm your only option." He smirks victoriously, removing his leather jacket.

My focus roams over him, taking in his black motorcycle boots, dark jeans, and a light-blue, button-down cotton shirt. He has the sleeves casually rolled up—showing off his tattoos.

In addition to the leather bracelets, he's wearing an expensive Breitling watch on his left wrist and a dark brown, beaded band on his right. I continue to stare at his jewelry, stalling.

He runs his hands over his face, trying to keep himself in check. "If you prefer, you could ride on the back of my bike into town, then we could call the tow company?"

Never take rides from strangers, Graysin! Even super-hot ones with expensive watches and sexy Celtic tattoos. I shake my head no. I'd rather drive myself into town. I pop open the trunk with a sigh.

If he kills me, so be it.

The stranger smiles brightly, chuckling as if he heard my thoughts. He walks around to the back of my car, and I listen as he moves my luggage around, before he lifts the floor cover, pulls out the jack, and begins lowering the spare.

I look around for the wolf, but there is no sign of it.

Guilt settles into my stomach. My savior is out there alone, in the pitch black, where a wild animal was just staring and growling at me. *Damn it.* I grab my keys, turning on my tiny keychain flashlight. There is no way he'll be able to see what he's doing without the light or my help.

Reluctantly, I open the door and slip out of the car. My boots hit the gravel with a crunch. I walk around to the front of my car and gasp at how much damage a few rocks did. The tire is shredded. It looks almost like it was slashed. A few seconds later, the Good Samaritan approaches, and I realize how tall he is compared to my five-foot-four frame; he has at least a foot on me.

He places the spare down and leans it against my car as he takes in the ruined tire.

"You must have done more damage to it when you skidded."

"I guess. It looks like something clawed at it."

"What were you avoiding? A bunny?" he teases.

My eyes slide to the area where the animal was. "A large, reddish wolf. Is that even possible?"

"Rusty," he whispers, with an annoyed huff.

"What?"

He stills, before speaking slowly. "Your rims look a little rusty," he points out. "And, yes, a wolf is possible. You're in the mountains now, city girl. Wild animals are abundant up here."

I shiver as the wind lifts again. "Right."

He falls silent before he bends down and begins to remove the old tire.

"We don't have a lot of wildlife in Newport, Rhode Island. I mean, other than the ocean life."

"I saw your license plate. Newport is home?"

"Yeah. All my life. You?"

"I live in Havenwood Falls, by way of Spain." His voice is tight. Not unfriendly, just guarded.

"Really?" I brighten at his confession. "What's it like?"

"Barcelona? Beautiful. Great food, people, and markets."

"I meant Havenwood Falls."

"Charming. Lots of festivals. Good coffee. Interesting characters. That sort of thing."

I hold the flashlight higher as he begins to put on the full-size spare. "This is my first visit."

He squints up at me, and a smug grin spreads over his perfect mouth, like he already knew.

"I'm staying at the Whisper Falls Inn while in town. I rented a cottage," I ramble.

The stranger falls silent as he goes back to replacing the tire. I stop speaking as I watch his every move, taking in his rugged good looks. A familiar sensation crosses over me as I focus on his broad shoulders. Every so often, the corded muscles make an appearance under his shirt.

"Hey, could you lower the light a bit? I've almost got this."

I squat next to him, and his gaze finds mine, prowling over me, causing my breath to catch. My chest begins to rise and fall rapidly as I try to pull air into my lungs, but it's not working.

"Easy." He leans closer. "You're at a higher altitude now. Slow down your breathing."

I inhale slowly through my nose, trying to push off a slight headache beginning to form.

"You need to be careful up here. If you aren't used to the high altitude, you'll get sick."

"Just another life change I'll have to get acclimated to, I guess."

After a few more intense moments pass between us, he finishes changing out the tire.

Once my breathing evens out, he stands and holds out his hand to help me up. Without a second thought, I slide my fingers across his palm and allow him to guide me to stretch to my full height.

"You okay?"

I nod.

"You should be all set now. I'll throw the damaged tire in your trunk. Once you're settled in town, swing by the Havenwood Falls Garage. Tell Joshua I sent you. He'll take good care of you." His accented voice is silky, calming.

I nod again, suddenly feeling shy and vulnerable. Averting from his, my gaze lands on our entangled hands, and I realize I'm still holding on to him. An unexpected blush rises on my cheeks, and I quickly remove my palm from his. My body shamelessly protests the action.

"S-sorry," I blurt out quickly, and wrap my arms around my stomach to avoid reaching out for him again. "Thanks. For fixing it. And stopping. And helping me breathe. You know," I babble, unable to stop. "All of it. Undressing and redressing me—it. The tire. Anyway . . . thanks."

He leans back on his heels, a haughty grin curling on his lips.

"No problem. You're lucky I couldn't sleep and was out for a late-night drive."

I open my mouth but nothing comes out. Not even air. Did I mention I'm socially awkward?

"All right then," he slowly draws out, in reply to my lack of response.

I watch as he picks up the tire, throws it into my trunk, and closes the hatch before I come to my senses. Shaking off my gawking, I quickly make my way to the driver's side, but he's faster and grabs the door for me, holding it open, waiting for me to slide in.

Once I do, he leans in closer.

So close that his mouth is only a breath from mine, and warm, mint-flavored air brushes over my lips. "Start her up. I'll follow you into town."

I raise my eyebrows at his statement.

"It's easy to get lost out here. I'll make sure you get to the inn safely."

"O-okay," is all I manage, as his spicy scent wraps around me, stupefying me.

His green eyes drill into me, searching my own.

"W-what did you say your name was?"

"Everett." His voice is husky.

"Graysin," I reply.

"Well, Graysin . . . welcome, to Havenwood Falls."

PURCHASE *COVETOUSNESS* at your favorite book retailer.

A Havenwood Falls New Adult Novella

HAVENWOOD
FALLS

FORGET
YOU
NOT

KRISTIE COOK

Forget You Not (**A Havenwood Falls Novella**) **by Kristie Cook**

Two years ago, Kaela Peters nearly killed her fiancé by ripping his throat out. Once she gained control over her vampire urges, she hoped to rekindle their love, only to find him on one knee again—now with her best friend. She can't blame them for their betrayal, though. They've been compelled to forget that she even existed. But she can't forget them, so when she receives an unexpected job offer far away in the Colorado mountains, she seizes the opportunity to escape her past and the painful memories.

If only she'd known she was running right into her true past and memories that cut even deeper.

Her real name isn't Kaela Peters, Havenwood Falls and her new job are not what they seem on the surface, and the love of her life isn't the ex in Atlanta. As she starts piecing together the fragmented memories of her past and her moroi heritage, the passion of old love reignites. Until she discovers that the triggering of her vampire gene may have been foul play with dire consequences—and Xandru Roca, the epic love she'd left behind, has something to do with it all.

FORGET YOU NOT

AN EXCERPT

othing screamed badass vampire chick more than hiding behind a menu while your ex-fiancé and former best friend sucked each other's faces three tables over and five booths down. I could hear their lips smacking and smell their horn-dog pheromones from my small table at the back of the restaurant. As if hiding wasn't pathetic enough, I couldn't stop stealing glances at them from over the top of the laminated cardboard in my hands, some sick part of me reveling in the painful twists of my heart and knots in my gut. *That's supposed to be me.* My eyes squeezed shut to suppress the threatening tears as I slid further down in my seat.

Ugh. I'm such a freakin' masochist.

"Kaela Peters, you are such a fucking masochist."

My eyes popped open at the sound of my roommate's raspy voice to find the redhead plopping down in the chair across from me, her green apron bunched up in one hand. One of her brows lifted as she stared at me with big, blue eyes, gnawing on her plump bottom lip, painted as scarlet as her hair. The color was all the more vibrant against her unnaturally porcelain-white skin. Sindi was also a vampire; in fact, in a much more traditional way than I was. Her coloring, for example —pale like vampires should be while my skin was still the olive tone it had always been. Her eyes had stayed the same, except when she fed from the vein, and then they sort of glowed, but mine made a permanent change from brown to a greenish-gray when I turned. We hadn't figured that one out.

After enduring several long moments of her glare, I finally shrugged and widened my eyes with as much innocence as I could muster. "What? It's not like I followed them here."

"Not this time."

My eyes began to drift over to the happy couple once more before I snapped them back to her. I didn't fool her, though. She noticed, if rolling her eyes was any indication.

"I guess you're at least taking my advice," she muttered as she unfolded her long legs and stood to tie her apron around her small waist. "But when the hell were you going to tell me?"

My brows pinched together at the sudden change in her tone, from snarky to … pained. It took a lot to hurt Sindi's feelings—her heart was possibly tougher than her indestructible body. Another of the differences between us. My body could heal itself in a short time; hers healed immediately. My skin burnt and blistered in the sun, but she'd burst into flames. I still needed oxygen (though not as much as a human), and she didn't. My heart still beat, while hers was silent. But could it still be broken? What could I have done to do so?

"I'm sorry," I said, "but tell you what?"

She blew out a quick breath. "It's okay, Kaela, I get it. When you joked about moving far away from here and your past, I was serious when I said you should. I'll miss you, but it's what you need. But don't lie to me about it."

"I really have no idea what you're talking about." Actually, muttering about moving away hadn't really been a joke, but not something I'd done anything about. Yet. My eyes stole another glimpse of the cuddling exes at the thought of leaving, and I sighed. I really was too much of a masochist.

Sindi's hands landed at her waist, and her long fingers tapped against her hip bones as she let out another huff. "Whisper Falls Inn? Job offer? You left the email open on your laptop this morning. How could you not even tell me that you'd applied? And Colorado? Really, Kaela? Do you know how long that drive from Atlanta would be? I can only drive at night! You couldn't find anything closer?"

I stared at her, confused. "Why wouldn't you fly?"

She rolled her eyes. "You know why."

I opened my mouth to ask because I had no idea why, but then shook my head. How she got to Colorado didn't matter.

"Unbunch your panties," I said instead. "I can't have a job offer. I haven't applied for anything new in ages. And definitely not in Colorado."

She glared at me for another long moment, and she must have seen the truth in my eyes because her baby blues began to soften and she started fiddling with the contents of her apron pocket. "Yeah, well, you shouldn't leave your shit out and open if you don't want me to know. But if you care at all about my opinion, I think it's pretty perfect for you. You should take it." She broke our eye contact as she glanced around the restaurant. "My shift's about to start. Where are you tonight?"

"Nowhere. I have the rare night off."

"Then get your ass home, and if you don't take that job, find another—a real one."

"Hey! You bartend and wait, too. You can't get any more real than those."

"*Those*. Multiple. When was your last day off? Three weeks ago? You really want to hold down two jobs for the rest of your very long life? And at a 24-hour, hole-in-the-wall diner and meat-market nightclub? You're too smart for this, Kae. Go use your degree, for Christ's sake." She turned and headed for the kitchen.

"Yeah, well, easier said than done. Not too many companies have night shifts for their PR teams."

I stood up and threw some money on the table, although I hadn't eaten anything. I *could* eat food. Blood sustained me, but I still loved food. Just not while watching the Ryan & Heather Sappy Love Show starring the two people who'd been my favorite souls in the world at one time. They still kind of were. Sindi had nudged them into second and third place, but I still loved them both. It wasn't their fault they'd fallen for each other. That was all on me.

"Sindi," I called out to her back as she retreated. She turned halfway and threw me an impatient look. It was all a cover, I knew. She'd never tell me I was one of *her* favorite people—she'd never open up enough to admit to that anyone—but she'd basically just shown it. "I'm not going anywhere. Relax."

"Don't worry about me, doll face. You do what you need to do. I will be fine. Always am." Her mouth curved up in a smirk before she tossed her red ponytail over her shoulder and disappeared between the swinging doors to the kitchen.

I headed down the corridor toward the bathrooms—and the back door. Although I hadn't permanently left the area in the two years since the night that changed my entire life, I'd been successful in avoiding running into *them*, and I didn't want to change that now. I might have sometimes (frequently) watched (stalked) from a distance, but the thought of actually coming anywhere close to Ryan or Heather sent me into panic mode. Sindi had compelled them both to forget me and everything that had happened between us, but unfortunately her vampire power didn't work on me, fellow vampire and all. I remembered it all—the good, the bad, and the very gruesome ugly.

The cool night air of winter in the South was a welcome relief as I slipped into the dark alley and headed home, thinking about how Sindi had been my saving grace when I'd been a newborn vampire. She'd found me in this very alley covered in blood. My fiancé's blood. Hence, the "ex" part of our relationship. I'd nearly killed him when I ripped half his throat out. Hey, I didn't know what I was doing. Seriously. We'd gone to sleep after making love, and I awoke a couple of hours later with a throat-searing thirst. Water just didn't cut it. I'd been overcome with bloodlust, although I didn't know that's what it was at the time.

Yep. I'd nearly murdered my fiancé. The night he'd proposed.

After taking care of him with the healing qualities of her own blood, Sindi whisked me away from civilization before I could kill anyone and taught me how to control the thirst. It took a while—and a lot of fights with Sindi and many nights locked up in her storage room to keep me from becoming a murderer—but I eventually grew to the point where animal blood sustained my body and actual human food satisfied my hunger. Once I knew I'd be okay, I thought I'd give the Ryan and Kaela Show another chance. But I was too late. He'd already moved on, of course. He'd moved right on top of my best friend. I couldn't blame either of them, though. After all, they didn't even know I existed. How could they know the betrayal I felt?

Once inside the townhouse Sindi and I shared—well, she shared with me since it was hers long before she met me—I found my laptop open on the coffee table in the living room. A swipe of the trackpad proved the truth of her story: on the screen was an open email. Weird. I hadn't seen it this morning. I dropped down onto the couch to read.

Dear Ms. Peters,

After reviewing your history and qualifications, we believe you are a perfect fit for the Night Manager position at Whisper Falls Inn in the beautiful mountains of Colorado, and we're excited to offer you the job. We have outlined the terms of employment, including compensation, below. If you agree with our conclusion, we would like you to start as soon as possible. We understand you may need time to consider our offer, but we hope you will respond quickly so we may start making preparations for your arrival.

Yours truly,

M. Luiza

The rest of the email outlined a modest salary enhanced by free lodging and meals but failed to provide any other details, such as an address or even city.

"Spam is getting weirder by the day," I muttered as I closed the email, cursing spammers and hackers. I wondered what this joker's end-game was. What did they get out of a fake job offer?

Not two seconds later, another message popped up, opening itself.

Ms. Peters,

We apologize that in our excitement of offering you the job, we failed to provide necessary details. Our inn is located in what we like to think of as the prettiest and most charming small town in the world. We are surrounded by majestic mountains and forestland with a larger variety of wildlife than anywhere else in the state, perhaps the country. While the area offers much to do, from skiing to hunting to art classes, we have safeguards in place that ensure our hometown remains a lovely place to live, not just to visit. We've attached a few pictures so you can see for yourself why we believe you will quickly learn to call it home and the people family.

Yours truly (again),

M. Luiza

A slideshow began to play at the bottom of the message, featuring gorgeous photos of a small town nestled in a cradle of purple mountains with snowcapped peaks.

"Awesome," I muttered as my hand moved the cursor to X out of the window. "Virus must already be installed."

My finger lowered over the trackpad and was about to press down when the slideshow displayed a photo that made my breath catch, and not because of its beauty. A large Victorian manor, complete with turrets and gingerbread trim, forced my pause. *How do I know that place?* The sense of familiarity poked angrily at the back of my mind. The photo changed, focused in on the plaque by the manor's front door: Whisper Falls Inn, Est. 1854.

Home.

The word floated through my mind, not as a premonition or wishful thinking as the letter promised, but heavily laced with nostalgia. The townhome's living room in front of me disappeared as other, seemingly random images hijacked my vision. Images of what could have been the rooms inside the inn, followed by portraits and snapshots of people. Faces that I felt deep down I should know. A close-up of a woman with long, dark hair like mine . . . gray-green eyes, the same shade and shape as mine.

Home.

"What the hell?" I slammed my finger down on the pad, closing out the message, and shut the laptop before jumping back in my seat, as though the message could hurt me. My heart raced, and I struggled to breathe. I curled into a ball on the couch and glared at the offensive machine on the coffee table. After several moments, my heart settled and everything returned to normal. Another few moments and I couldn't remember what had caused such a visceral reaction. "I'm losing my damn mind."

Sindi had warned me about vampires losing their sanity, but always in relation to being starved of blood. I was not starved of blood, nor of food. Well, I didn't eat earlier. I unfolded myself from the sofa and headed for the kitchen to find something for . . . I glanced at the clock on the stove. 11:48 p.m. Something for brunch.

As I cooked and ate, my mind wandered back to Sindi's orders and the fake job offer. Maybe it wasn't real, but it got me to thinking. Hotel night manager wasn't exactly what I'd had in mind when I switched my major from pre-med to business after I'd turned and then continued with night classes to earn my event planning certification, thinking event planners worked at night. They did, but, turned out, not *only* at night. But maybe there was potential here. After all, hotels hosted events and many at night. I'd taken the bartending job to grow into a special events planner at the club, but it'd been more than a year and that had gone nowhere. And this was a full-time, salaried position with benefits in a place so far away, it didn't get reception for the Ryan & Heather Super Sappy Love Show.

The small-town part, though . . . I'd come to Atlanta in the first place to escape the small-town life of my childhood. I'd done quite well in putting that misery behind me, never thinking about home and the family that had taken me in only because they had to, but didn't really want me. I'd escaped that life once. Did I really want to go back? Of course, the pictures of the mountain village looked nothing like the dusty Texas town where I'd grown up. Maybe Colorado small towns were different.

"Yeah, right." I dropped my plate in the dishwasher and cleaned up the rest of the kitchen before sitting down to clean up my computer.

After the virus scan came back clean, I went on an online hunt for a new job—hotel night manager. Every single listing I found on every single job site was the same one: Whisper Falls Inn.

PURCHASE *FORGET You Not* at your favorite book retailer.

www.ingramcontent.com/pod-product-compliance
Lightning Source LLC
Chambersburg PA
CBHW052013170626
46808CB00007B/2902